To: Olivia

DA[illegible]

MW01265076

NIGHT

The Story of Tucker and Shiloh in the Civil War

As told by:

TUCKER: A Horse in the U.S. Mounted Infantry

and

SHILOH: a Horse in the Confederate Volunteer Cavalry

Put Down in Words By:

From: Mattie Richardson

Mattie Richardson

Keep telling stories!! ☺

Day and Night

First Printing*April 2015

ISBN: 978-0-9838171-4-7

Additional copies of this book and other books by Mattie Richardson are available by mail. Please see the back of the book for an order form.

Published by: Mattie Richardson
www.facebook.com/appaloosy7

Printed in the USA by
Morris Publishing®
3212 East Highway 30
Kearney, NE 68847
1-800-650-7888

This book is dedicated to:

Kaye Lervold Cover

A wonderful teacher, fellow author, mother and grandmother, and a great friend.

Once a stranger, now my favorite fan. Thank you so much for all your support and encouragement.

There is many a war-horse who is more entitled to immortality than the man who rides him.

–GENERAL ROBERT E. LEE

Civil War-era words and terms used in this book:

Bushwhacker: a Confederate guerilla before and during the Civil War. Bushwhackers often organized raids against rural families considered to be sympathetic to Union causes, but they also burned towns and committed other acts of violence.

Confederates, Gray-backs, Rebs, Johnny Reb: All nicknames and names used in this book for Confederate soldiers.

Dixie; Dixieland: A nickname for the Confederate south.

Free-Soilers: This term was used for a political party during the time of the Civil War that opposed slavery and the expansion of slavery into new states and territories. Many of the people who believed in the ideas of the party became known as Free Soilers as well, even if they weren't officially in the political party.

General Order 11: Issued by Union General Thomas Ewing in 1863, this order demanded that all people in a few western counties of Missouri needed to evacuate the area, regardless of their allegiance. It came about because of the violence of the bushwhackers.

Hardtack: Hardtack was an especially hard, dry kind of bread or biscuit that soldiers often ate as rations during the Civil War.

Jayhawker: The same as a bushwhacker, but the word was more often used for guerilla fighters from Kansas.

Stars and Bars: A nickname for the Confederate flag

Union, Yankees, Blue-coats, Feds: All names and nicknames used for Union soldiers in this book.

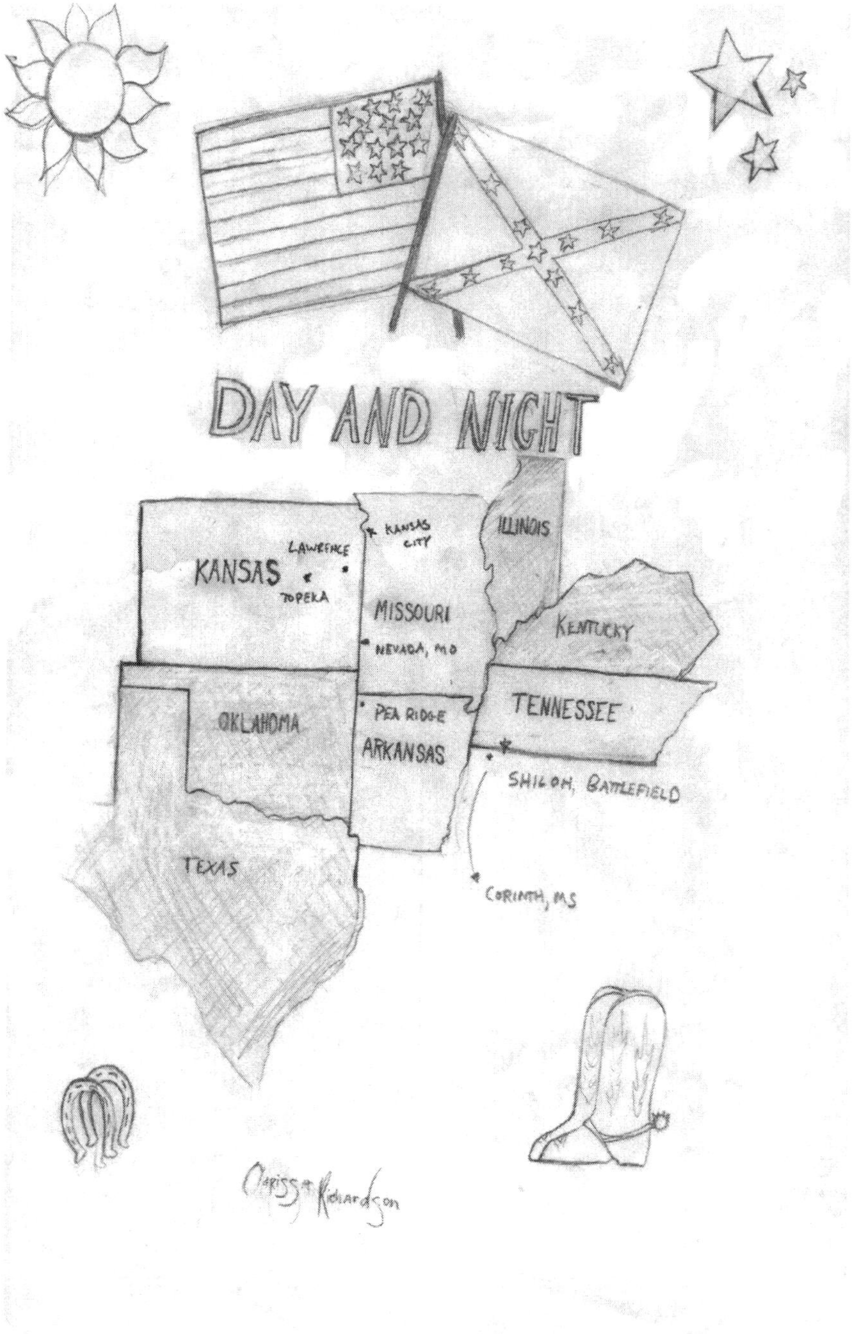
DAY AND NIGHT
KANSAS
LAWRENCE
TOPEKA
KANSAS CITY
MISSOURI
NEVADA, MO
ILLINOIS
KENTUCKY
TENNESSEE
OKLAHOMA
PEA RIDGE
ARKANSAS
SHILOH, BATTLEFIELD
TEXAS
CORINTH, MS
Clarissa Richardson

Shiloh – Fall of 1861

"Watch out, Tucker!" I yelled as I reared, then galloped over the tangle of prairie grass toward my older brother. He didn't move but neighed a challenge to me, and I slammed into him from the side. He rolled over on the ground but was up again in a minute, pinning his ears and good-naturedly snapping at me.

The wind blew across the Missouri prairie playfully, tossing about our lengthy forelocks and manes as we fought. We could hear the sound of the creek not far away, rushing over the large chunks of granite and limestone that had been in the area since the beginning of time. The sun was shining gracefully and the air had yet to become as cool as it probably should have been in September.

My brother Tucker was a three year-old; I wasn't two yet but I tested his patience nonetheless and loved play-fighting with him.

Both he and I had been born on a small farm in Missouri, and we were both Morgan horses of the best bloodlines going back to the great Justin Morgan horse himself. Our mother was one of the best mares owned by a man named Casey, who owned and cared for us as well.

The lush green pasture was our playground, where we galloped, bucked and fought as colts.

Tucker had beat me up pretty good and was chasing me toward the little creek that ran through our pasture, and I barely had time to stop before I skidded into the water and fell right on my nose.

I pulled myself out of the cold water and shook, trying to rid myself of the water that ran down my coat. Tears welled up in my little eyes, but as I turned to look at Tucker I saw him laughing!

I stomped out of the creek, infuriated.

I had always felt a little challenged by my older brother. He had the good looks and athleticism that Casey was looking for in his Morgan horses, for sure. As he stood laughing at me, again I noticed his shimmering dark brown bay coat with sharp, contrasting black markings, his tall form and well-muscled outline.

I had no such features; one could hardly tell that we were brothers. My speckled gray coat was rather drab, my mane seemed to be always tousled and I had always been on the shorter side, little more than fourteen hands when I stretched to my full height. My mother always said that we were as different as day and night.

"Boys!" my mother scolded when she found us fighting again. "Settle down, or one of you is surely going to get hurt!"

She trotted up beside us and straightened out my mane. "Shiloh, you need to stop taunting your older brother."

"I am not!" I protested.

"And Tucker," she said, "you know better than to tease Shiloh."

Tucker just laughed and trotted up to me to rub noses. "I love Shiloh, even if I do pick on him too much. You know that, right Shiloh?"

I shook and jumped away from him defiantly. "That lovey-dovey stuff won't work on me." But really, I was glad to know that my brother cared for me, even if he did pick on me. Tucker's eyes softened and he smiled before he trotted away to find some tougher horses in the pasture to play with. I sighed and began to trot away as well but my mother came up behind me and stopped me.

I halted when I felt her stop beside me. She gently rested her nose on top of my withers and closed her eyes for a second. I twisted my neck around to look at her.

"You know your brother cares about you, even if he teases you," she said softly. I looked at her curiously, wondering why she was paying me such attention. She was quiet for a moment. "Casey is downsizing his herd," she told me. "He's considering moving north because of the problems that we've been having lately with the border ruffians. All the young horses are going to be sold."

I started. How did she know this?

"But…I won't be able to see you or Tucker or any of the other horses again, will I? Especially if he sells us all separately."

She arched her neck and raised her nose to meet mine. "Most likely. You may never even see any of us again," she said sadly. "But it is all a part of growing up, my dear Shiloh."

Tucker

A lot of different men came to look at Casey's horses, as they were known all around for being some of the finest Justin Morgan horses in the area. Casey had about fifteen head of horses, and he planned on selling most of them and only keeping a few for himself. Tensions were rising in the North and the South over issues of slavery and state's rights, and there had even been bullets shot at Fort Sumter, or so we had heard.

I was only a three year-old at the time, so I didn't pay particular attention to all of the details. I just remember Casey coming into the pasture with another man I had never seen before. Casey was somewhat on the shorter side, an older man with years of wisdom that he used in breeding and selling his horses.

The man he was with was younger and taller, with blond hair; maybe in his late twenties.

"I have a lot of good horses, but this one is one of the best," Casey was telling him. "He's not broke yet, but he's as fast as the wind. Name's Tucker, and when you watch him gallop across the pasture you'll see he's got the beauty of Pegasus."

I blew air through my nose and snorted nervously when they approached, but I didn't move and allowed Casey to loop the rope around my neck, then work to tie the halter around my face. He led me out of the pasture, and the other men followed behind, watching me carefully as I followed Casey.

He had a bit of a smile on his face, which I liked. He looked like a kind man, not too rough. Casey let out the slack in the rope and flicked the end of it at me, and I trotted around him in a small circle, allowing the other man to see how well I moved.

Casey allowed me to stop, and I walked up to him. He scratched my neck, and said to the man, "So, how do you like him?"

The man nodded silently, then held up his hand to my nose and tenderly rubbed it.

"Alright then," Casey said. "Tucker, meet Jordan."

Jordan mounted his horse and took my lead rope from Casey. "Thank you very much, Mr. Harris," Jordan told Casey. "I can't wait to begin working with him!"

Jordan kicked his horse and the horse took off at a trot, and I quickly followed before my head was yanked. My ears swiveled left and right as I took in my surroundings one more time before I left the place that had been my home for the last three years. Across the rolling hills of the pasture, the bright white barn, and Casey's house, and the other horses that were still in the pasture.

I saw a gray figure gallop frantically to the edge of the fence near where we were trotting by; Jordan was in front riding his horse and ponying me close behind.

Shiloh galloped to meet us at the end of the fence, his short form rushing toward us in order to say one last quick goodbye. He whinnied loudly. I looked back one more time and neighed back to him. I didn't know if I would ever be able to see my brother again.

This Jordan fellow must have been really interested in buying a fine Morgan horse, as he had traveled quite a distance to find one. He rode all day and well into the night before stopping at a small house. The fading light of the end of the day made it too dark for me to make out most of the details of the place where Jordan lived, but I could see a house, a little gray shed, and the pasture.

Jordan stopped, dismounted and led his horse, an older chestnut mare I learned was named Willow. I followed close behind. He unsaddled Willow and then led her with her bridle on one side of him, and me on the other. When we got to the gate he released Willow into the pasture first, then let me go to follow her.

Jordan allowed me a few days to get used to the place before he began to work with me. At daybreak the next day I was able to look around and found myself on a small farm that was located in eastern Kansas. There were plenty of cattle in the other pasture, but Willow and I were the only two horses. Willow was a kind mare as I soon found out, and she was used mostly for the work around the farm but Jordan had been looking for a younger horse to take over.

Soon after daybreak two small children ran out to the pasture, followed by Jordan.

"Papa, is this the new horse you got?" asked the smaller one, a little girl with yellow hair and a dirty light blue dress.

"Boy, he's a beauty," the older one, a small tan boy of maybe ten years, commented. He whistled. "And tall, too."

"Yep," said Jordan, "His name is Tucker. He's going to be the new work horse around here. If he's really good, then I'll let you ride Willow, Tommy."

The boy, Tommy, smiled hugely when he heard that.

The two children came to watch as Jordan made an effort to break me in. He wanted to start working with me as soon as possible. The kids sat on the edge of the corral as they watched their father chase me around in circles to tire me out before he attempted to saddle me.

Though I had never been trained to ride yet, I had seen the other horses around Casey's place being broken in by Casey's gentle hand before. I was used to and knew what a saddle and bridle were like.

But that didn't mean I was ready for it. I shied the first time Jordan showed me the saddle and ran to the other side of the small corral, scaring the little girl and causing her to jump off from where she was sitting. But Jordan talked to me calmly and approached me again.

This time he got the saddle blanket on my back and then gently put the saddle on top of it. I stood still but my eyes were a little wide at the unaccustomed weight that was on my back. Before I knew it he was on my left side and had tightened up the cinch to hold the saddle in place. He backed away and smiled. I raised my head and looked around, confused.

"Come on, Tucker fellow," Jordan said quietly. "Walk on over here."

How was I supposed to do that? It felt so strange having the heavy western saddle cinched to my back. But I took one small step, then another. Some instinct in me snapped, and I began to run around the corral, crow-hopping and bucking all along the way to see if I could get the saddle off. Jordan kept his cool and stood in the center of the corral, saying nothing and only watching me until I calmed down.

When I was assured that the heavy thing on my back wouldn't hurt me, I stopped. Jordan smiled again and approached me, scratching my neck with his kind hand. "That a boy, Tucker," he said. "It's alright."

It was right about that time when Jordan's two dogs began to bark, and Jordan and I turned to look at a man riding towards the corral.

He dismounted and looped his horse's reins around one of the boards of the corral. "Hullo, Jordan," he said quietly. "Thank you so much for the use of your nippers and file. I've brought them back to you. One of these days I will get around to getting my own pair."

Jordan smiled at the man and walked over to the edge of the corral where he stood. "No problem, Will. Borrow them whenever you need to."

The man, Will, stood and looked at me in the corral for a moment. "Nice horse you have there. Where did you get that one?"

"Casey Harris, just across the border in Missouri. He's a real fine horse, isn't he?"

"Definitely," the man agreed. "But Casey? Isn't he one of those Rebels?"

Jordan scowled. "Yes, I think he is siding with the south. But I ain't going to hold it against him. I've found that if I just keep my nose out of the whole business that people will leave me alone."

"Not true, my friend," Will countered. "Tensions are risin' everywhere. The abolitionists are stirring up a storm, and the Rebels are ready to fight back. You remember how the Southerners sent voters flocking into Kansas to make sure that it would be entered into the union as a slave state?"

Jordan nodded grimly. "Yes, I remember. But they can't do anything to me. If I just keep to myself and stay away from all that fiery political talk it'll be alright."

"Jordan!" the man said, "if you are not for or against anything, both sides will be against you. You need to make up your mind and at least stick with it. I've heard things are getting violent. Killings, raidings, things getting stolen left and right. Some stolen right from people's own neighbors. Life is getting even more complicated in Kansas, there's talk of a full-out war. And not the short-lived war that we expected—this war could last a year or more. A lot of settlers are moving out."

Jordan said nothing but nodded, then took hold of my halter and began to unsaddle me.

Later that night, I talked to Willow about the things I had heard in Jordan's conversation.

She nodded. "It's true. Things are getting difficult in these parts. I almost think that Jordan should move out, since he has no strong feelings toward either side of the war. He could get caught in the middle of some tricky business."

"So what is it that they're really fighting about?" I asked curiously.

"Well," she replied, "Kansas and Nebraska have just entered the Union not too long ago on the basis of a thing called 'popular sovereignty' which means the settlers themselves will decide whether the state will be a slave state or free, rather than have the men in the capital decide. Well, it turns out that is harder that it seems. People thought that it would be a free state because it was so far north. But Border Ruffians from Missouri and other southern states poured into Kansas to vote to make Kansas a slave state. I believe that eventually it was brought in as a free state, and though that may solve problems on paper it does nothing for the state's internal violence. There are even two state capitals set up in Kansas, one slave and one free. I'm not sure exactly what's going on, but I do know that we're in for a mess of trouble."

I looked up at the night sky, trying to understand all that Willow had told me. She may have been an old horse, but she was wiser than any other I had known.

The night was cool with a pleasant breeze blowing from the west. Stars lit up the sky and there was a full moon out, perfectly lighting the pasture so that I could see Willow as I talked to her.

"So, isn't that it?" I asked her. "Shouldn't the fighting be done now? I mean, it wasn't fair of them to come in from other states to vote, but it isn't like there are a lot of slaves here in Kansas anyway."

She shook her sorrel head. “It should be. But the ‘Free Soilers’ are choosing to ignore the new government and set up one of their own. It’s some tricky business. The fights are getting worse too. It’s just not over the matter of slave states or free, the whole union is in trouble.” She lowered her voice. “Some people say that it’s not even just about the little border fights anymore. There are whisperings of a nation-wide Civil War.”

It was another such night that Willow and I stood quietly in the pasture. Willow grazed quietly and I was between sleep and dreamy awareness, thinking about life. I had really come to like Jordan. He was a kind master and took care of Willow and me well. He had completely broken me in to ride and was working on training me to drive. I didn’t mind; I liked it when he took me out in the early hours before it got too hot to ride. We rode down beside the river and up through the little patch of forest, and I relished the quiet adventure every morning.

Learning to drive would be fun too. Jordan had a nice little buggy he used to go to church on Sundays and to town when he could. Pulling it was a breeze, and it was fun to race across the hard-packed prairie road with Jordan behind me.

Willow suddenly raised her head and looked off into the distance, and I did the same. I thought I heard something as she had. Willow trotted over to the edge of the fence to get a better look and I followed her.

I could definitely hear something in the forest. I looked at Willow nervously but she just looked into the darkness, her eyes following the shadows of something in the distance. Suddenly I saw it too. Horsemen were approaching, a fairly good-sized group of about a dozen or more.

I was curious, but a little scared at the same time. What would a group of riders be doing here in the middle of the night? They rode up to the house and I heard them bang on the door. Hearing no answer, they kicked in the door and burst inside the house. I trotted around nervously, wondering what was going on, but Willow stood tall and just watched silently.

Shortly after I saw them bring out Jordan, followed by his wife and his two children. Some of the men were still in the house rummaging around and making a ton of noise, while a small group of the men led Jordan and his family close to the barn.

I could see and hear them better when they got closer to the pasture, and I saw that all of the men held Sharp's rifles at their sides.

"I don't know what you think you're doing!" Jordan told them desperately. "I'm not for either side. I'm peaceful and all I want to do is farm and raise my family here in Kansas."

One of the men pushed him to the ground. He was a tall, heavyset man with dark hair and a long dark moustache to match. "We've been told differently. It's been said that you're sympathetic to Southern causes." He spat on the ground next to Jordan.

Willow moved beside me. "I don't know who they are for sure. They could be either Free-Soilers or Jay-Hawkers," she whispered.

"How can you go off just what you heard?" Jordan asked angrily. The little girl clung to her mother and tears fell down her cheeks, and Tommy glared at the man defiantly.

"It's common knowledge, you scum."

The men were coming out of the house and more were making their way into the barn. One more man came into the pasture and looped a halter around Willow and did the same to me. Both of us were brought near the man who stood talking to

Jordan and his family. A man was loading bags of feed onto a mule and another was bringing the horses back.

The man mounted his tall horse and glared down at Jordan and his family in disgust. "You should be happy with us. We are content to take your belongings and leave your farm intact. We aren't like those Bushwhackers who massacre and burn people's farms and houses. But this better teach you a lesson about supporting any Rebel cause."

And with that, the men turned and rode away into the darkness, taking all of Jordan's belongings as well and Willow and me with them.

Shiloh

I didn't know what I would do without my brother at first. We were always together, he was my best friend, and now all I had was a bunch of other old horses and my mother. Until Casey sold my mother too. I guess he was moving somewhere else to get out of the area, since things were getting prickly with all the Jayhawkers and general lawbreakers in the area, but he didn't have to go and tear my whole family apart.

Well, I suppose that's what humans are for. Here to raise us, train us, sell us, use us to any advantage that they see fit. But it's our place in the world, as my mother told me, and we should be content to be there.

Casey wasn't able to sell me right away. I mean, who wants a short little gray horse who's slow and doesn't listen well? I wasn't slow just because I was short, I was sure I could outrun most of the horses on the farm if someone would give me a chance to.

Since Casey couldn't get the price he wanted for me right away, he began to work with me himself. I was two years old, after all, and the only horse that was really worth anything was a broke one.

He took me out to the corral and tied me to a sturdy post outside of it. I didn't like being tied up and I pulled back at first. Not like the other horses pulled back, like a little tease, but then giving up and maybe chewing contently on a piece of fence.

I reared up in the air and pulled back with all of my weight until a frayed piece of rope snapped. If you think you've seen chaos, wait until you see a thousand-pound horse thrashing around like he's having a seizure with a fly up his nose! Casey was just walking out of the barn when the rope broke, and I fell backwards right onto my haunches. I grunted and stood up quickly, regained my composure, then turned and ran for all I was worth.

I didn't really think that I was going to get anywhere by running, but if there's one thing I've taken the time to learn from other horses, it's how to avoid work. At least for a little while anyway. Casey shook his head and took out another horse to saddle and came to get me.

After two hours or so of chasing me around, he finally got a hold of the part of the rope that was hanging from my chin. He brought me back to the corral and tied me up in the same place that I was before. His next mistake.

He patted the saddle blanket on my back and I shied away at first, but then calmed down and let him place it on my back. Next he put the saddle on me, but I didn't move. I mean, what choice did I have? He reached for the bridle next. Uh-oh. It wasn't there. He'd have to go back to the barn to get it. "You stay here, you rotten horse," he said to me, almost under his breath. If I could have smiled at him I would have. I was determined to make this as hard for him as I could. I jumped up in the air again and threw my weight against the rope. But this time it was here to stay. I felt a weakness in it somewhere though. I continued to pull back and began to shake my head violently to the left and right. When Casey heard me thrashing around again he peeked his head out of the barn to see me pull the entire post out of the ground, get spooked and start running again, the post dragging behind me.

That was pretty much the end of my "training" for the day.

It was close to midnight, and I stood out in the pasture alone. The wind blew gently through my tangled mane as I trotted down toward the creek for a drink, and the stars shone like a million sparks throughout the night sky. I reached my muzzle down to the cool, crystal-clear water for a drink. My tender muzzle splashing in the water was the only noise in the cool night. I shook my head, and turned to look behind me. I could have sworn I heard another noise.

I suddenly saw a dark figure make its way along the fence line. My ears twisted curiously in its direction, and I couldn't help myself, I trotted towards it. I reached my head across the fence and found out that it was another human. That's funny, Casey didn't have any neighbors close by, and not a lot of people traveled through these parts.

"Curiosity's what killed the cat," they claim, and before I knew it, this man had a rope around my neck. He jumped inside the fence line and began to lead me toward the gate. I stalled; I didn't know who this man was or where he was taking me. But he slapped a crop hard against my rump and I jumped ahead. He led me to the gate, and opened it as quietly as he could.

I realized what was happening. This man was stealing me from Casey. I could see horses in the trees ahead and I whinnied a greeting. The man covered my nose, with a harsh *shhhhhh*! He brought me to the group of horses. Some of the horses standing there were what was left of Casey's small herd and there were also a couple mules.

"Did you get 'em all?" another man asked as soon as we were in the group.

The man that held my rope smiled. "This is the last one."

More men emerged from out of the night and mounted their horses. The man looped the rope around his saddle horn and kicked his horse into a lope and the rest followed.

The group of men kept riding throughout the night and onward through the next couple days, mostly taking low paths that were well hidden from the main road and stopping at a few farms to gather more horses and livestock, leaving other farms untouched. It was a tiring journey, but the men kept us moving at a fast pace. On the third day of traveling, as the first rays of sunlight made its way over the Missouri horizon, we arrived at a large ranch.

The men herded the horses into a large corral and let us go.

"Wow, you sure got a lot of them," an older man said as he made his way toward the horses.

"Spoils of war, I suppose," said the other man. "These horses and mules will be taken over to the base by Springfield."

"Good work, Aaron," he replied. "Our boys need these fine animals."

Aaron climbed up on top of the fence to get a better look at the horses. "I'm going to keep that one for myself, though." He said. "You see that speckled gray one? The short one, yes. I don't know why, he just kind of grew on me. I don't know if he's broke yet but it won't be a hard job."

"Well, go git 'im," the man said. "And go home and get some sleep. And be safe."

Aaron came to get me again. I let him catch me, I was too tired to fight him this time. He brought me out of the corral and back to his horse, where he looped the rope around his saddle horn again and kicked his horse into a trot.

It didn't take too long to get to where he lived. Turns out he was a single man and lived in a bunkhouse with some other men who helped work a farm. But he didn't plan on staying there for long. He had enlisted in the army and was planning on heading out to the battlefield soon.

I couldn't care less, and made myself at home with the other horses. Aaron was excited to work with his new mount though and had me in a small corral the next day. I was ready to put up a fight, as usual.

He got the saddle blanket, saddle and bridle on without much of a problem. It's just when he climbed aboard that I had a breakdown. I jumped into the air with a giant leap, and squealed, kicked out, and he was launched out of the saddle and was on the ground in less than a minute.

He stood up painfully and dusted off his pants. "Okay, then," he said. "You obviously haven't been worked with yet. But that's okay. I'll have you kid-broke within the day."

Aaron caught me and climbed aboard again. I bucked, crowhopped and jumped side to side, kicking up dust and successfully tossing him off my back again. I rushed to the other side of the fence and neighed to the other horses, begging for their attention.

But Aaron had lost his temper by this time. He stood up again, a dark scowl on his face as he turned toward me. "Alright then horse, it's time for the hard way now," he yelled at me. "Git your horse butt over here and I'm going to show you what it is to obey." I could sense that he was getting angry and that maybe it was time to settle down before things got out of hand. I turned to face him, the long split reins dragging on the ground.

He grabbed one and jerked it towards him, causing the sharp metal bit to split open the corner of my mouth. I followed him as he roughly led me back to the hitching post. From there he tied me up and began his work. He wrapped a heavy rope around my back hoof and up through the saddle horn, then pulled it tight, causing my hind foot to nearly touch my stomach. He tied it in a secure knot and left it there. He then took the reins and somehow attached it to a ring in the cinch under my stomach. My head was effectively pulled down in between my front legs. Altogether it made for an extremely uncomfortable position to hold.

"There!" he said with a satisfied air. "Let's see how you like that."

Okay. If he wanted to play the waiting game—bring it on.

By the next day, though, sweat rolled down my back, over the tops of my ears down my forelock and into my eyes. Dried blood had crusted over the side of my mouth, and all my muscles ached. I had been standing there tied up for hours, without anything to eat or drink, while Aaron attended to his other needs.

When he had finally come back, my muscles felt like they were on fire. I had been standing in the same place, in the same position, for more than twenty-four hours. I had managed to loosen the ropes a little, but with his iron-like knots the ropes were fairly immobile.

"Feelin' better today?" he asked me as he came near the corral. He loosened my head first but left my foot where it was. He led me, limping along behind him, into the coral. Here he climbed into the saddle again, breathing in quietly and then exhaling slowly. Then he dug his spurs into my sides.

My whole entire body shook with exhaustion, and I could barely move with my hind foot tucked up underneath my stomach. I fought the urge to simply lie down and give up, even with the man on my back. But I took a large breath in myself. And then I exploded.

I bucked the best I could, attempting to shake my foot loose in the process. I wasn't very successful at it, but Aaron was getting better at staying in the saddle. Either that or I was getting worse at getting him off. A few men had gathered around to watch what was going on as I kicked, lunged and bucked, kicking up dust as I flew around the coral. I finally fell to my knees on the ground before breaking my hoof loose. Then I let out all my fury. But Aaron still stayed on my back, until finally I jumped into the air with a giant rear. But my foot was too weak to hold me up. I fell backwards and crashed into the fence behind me. Pieces of fence exploded around me and Aaron fell with a sickening crack underneath me. I felt a surge of pain as a giant splinter forced its way through a tender muscle in my lower hind leg.

But I didn't have time to stop now. I got up and ran, a trail of blood following behind me.

It didn't take the humans too long to catch me again. One of the men who worked on the farm wanted to take care of my leg right away. But Aaron wouldn't let him. "Serves the horse right," he said, and left me in the corral for the night.

I just sat and sulked. I had heard the men talking. They said that a horse that acted like I did ought to be shot. Especially with my hind leg being the way it was. I didn't know what was going to happen to me, and frankly, I didn't care. I didn't have any friends and even the humans I was with were cruel.

I know that Tucker and my mother would have been disappointed with me, though. I know what they would have said. "What a waste of horse."

I stood quietly in the pasture into the night as I thought about things, but I didn't feel like eating. I simply tucked my head between my knees, depressed.

I raised it up again real quick when I heard another noise. It couldn't be Aaron coming to get me. It wasn't any of the any men.

You have got to be kidding me.

I saw a short, cloaked figure approaching with a rope in his hands. Maybe it was one of the men secretly coming out to doctor my poor foot. That would have been nice. But yet again I was to be stolen.

The figure jumped over the fence with the agility of a deer, and had that rope tied over my face in an instant. I didn't have the morale to fight. The figure led me out the gate, quiet as a mouse, and mounted his horse. And once again we trotted into the night.

This person led me a little farther down the road, a couple miles maybe, until we got to another little cabin. He dismounted his horse and made his way behind me, looking at my leg. "Dang—that leg is really bad." His voice was so quiet. He made his way up to the front of me, and lowered his hood to his shoulders, exposing two long yellow-blonde braids and sparkling blue eyes. "You're Confederate property now," she said with a smile. It wasn't another man.

I had been stolen once again. This time by a young woman.

Tucker

Willow and I traveled south and west with the men, following the great Missouri River, until we finally arrived at somewhat of a military camp that appeared to be in the middle of nowhere. It wasn't a very big camp, with maybe a hundred men in all. Fires were burning, some men were cooking food over them, a few played cards, yet others groomed or cared for horses.

The men brought us forward to a man sitting at a table, scribbling furiously in a book with an inked pen. "Hey, Kellerman," one of the men said. Kellerman, as he was called, looked up from his writing. The man dismounted his horse, and grabbed me by the halter and dragged me forward.

"I heard the Union is looking for horses."

"This is true," Kellerman replied.

"And they're payin' good prices. I've got a really nice bunch here that were taken from some Rebs."

Kellerman stood up, and took a quick glance at the dozen or so head of horses that were now standing around his table. His eye caught mine, and I snorted cautiously. He walked up to me and put a hand on my neck reassuringly. "Easy, boy."

The man holding my bridle backed away, and Kellerman smoothed his hand over my neck, and up towards my ears. He took a look into one of them, and I pulled away, but he pulled my head back toward him and pushed a thumb in my mouth to get me to open it. He took a good long look at my teeth, then backed away to look at me overall.

He whistled. “This here is a great horse,” he said. “Perfect for a cavalry or artillery mount. The other ones will do, too, but I really like this one.”

“How ‘bout two hundred for that one, and a hundred-fifty or so for the rest?” the man asked eagerly.

“Can’t do it,” Kellerman replied. “You know that we are not supposed to pay more than $140 a head.”

The man grumbled, but decided on taking it, as he said, “I’m doing it for the cause.”

After the money was exchanged, Kellerman led me back to where a lot of horses were tied. I took a good look around myself, snorted, and shoved aside some hay that was spread for the horses to eat. The man smiled, watching me for a moment, and then left.

I took the opportunity to talk to some of the other horses around me. I looked at a small paint mare beside me, and nickered softly. She looked up.

I smiled. “Do you know any more about this place than I do?” I asked, curious for more information.

She shook her double-colored forelock out of her eyes. “Sure do,” she replied. “Welcome to the Second Missouri cavalry regiment. Horses like you and I are being bought by the dozens to supply mounts for the cavalry.”

“Wow. This war is getting real.”

“Of course it is real. There was already a battle out east in Virginia, called the Battle of Bull Run—or Manassass. The Rebs are getting organized, it’s about time we did too.”

“Who exactly is ‘we’?” I asked, curious.

“Why, the Union forces, of course!” She replied. “We’re getting ready to put those Rebs back in their place.”

“Hmmm,” I thought out loud. I had heard of some of these things before, but I still didn’t know all the details. “Do they treat us well here?”

"Mainly, they do," she said, "at more than a hundred dollars a head, they can't really afford to mistreat their mounts. We are worked hard, but it's mostly drilling. The worst you will get here is a man who doesn't know how to ride."

I laughed. "A man who doesn't know how to ride? How can that even be?"

"You'll see," she replied, with a bit of a smirk.

The next morning as the sun was barely shining above the horizon, I heard a bugle scratching out from somewhere in the distance.

The paint mare beside me shook her mane and stretched out, yawning and exposing her large yellow teeth. "Wake-up call," she informed me.

I raised my head and perked my ears. What did that mean?

Our surroundings were beautiful. Large colored leaves fell silently from the trees and onto the ground as the autumn weather touched the southern Missouri landscape with a light, cold finger. Some of the leaves were as large as dinner plates and others small enough to fit in the palm of a man's hand. But it was the colors that were truly magnificent. There was bright orange, yellow, red and a few tinges of green. The camp soon came alive with men exiting the small beige tents, stirring campfires and preparing a breakfast of canned meat, hardtack and coffee. I watched them bustling around for awhile until another bugle called.

The paint mare stood up straighter. "'Boots and Saddles' call," she said. "Won't be long until they come for us."

I looked around myself excitedly. I wondered what was going to happen. I would soon learn. The men that made up the Volunteer Cavalry moved to their horses and began currying and brushing them, some putting on their spurs or their horses' saddles.

A young man with curly brown hair moved beside me, along with a general.

"This is the horse that will be for your use, Ben," the general said. "But only if you care for him properly. He's a mighty fine horse, and well-trained, too, so you shouldn't have many problems with him."

"Yes sir," Ben replied shortly. The general nodded to him and left.

I snorted cautiously. "It's alright, boy," he said to me. Ben was tall, clean shaven with brown curly hair and matching brown eyes, dressed in an oversized blue coat and pants. From his rough hands, I could tell that he was used to working hard, and I figured that he had probably done farm work before and had experience in riding and caring for horses, unlike what the paint mare had said.

He grabbed a brush and started combing out my shining bay coat. He seemed to be pretty good with horses, better than the few of the other men who seemed to struggle to get the saddle blankets on correctly and cinch up the saddles. He worked slowly and steadily, relaxing me by talking to me as he brushed my coat.

"I wonder where you're from," he said softly, almost more to himself than to me. "Were you a farm horse? Born and raised for a life of hard work? Trust me, this job is not going to be any less difficult, but certainly more noble."

He threw the saddle blankets up on my back, followed by the government-issued saddle. He cinched it up, pulled a bridle over my ears, and mounted. "Ready for morning drills?" he asked, and kicked me towards the gathering group of horses.

There were dozens, maybe even a hundred horses in the cavalry unit. The men lined up their horses, some with a bit of difficulty, and awaited the drill signals. I was glad to find that Ben had lined me up beside the little paint mare.

The bugle called out again, and the horses moved forward. I looked around myself but Ben guided me. This mysterious language that the soldiers used! As if English was not difficult enough, they had to be summoned by a bugle call as well. Move forward, come about halt. I made it more difficult on myself by trying to anticipate the moves and only stumbling into other horses. Ben was frustrated, but corrected me gently.

The paint mare leaned her mouth toward me. "Don't act like it's that hard," she scolded. "It's really not."

"But—"

She interrupted me. "Listen to the bugle," she whispered. "There's a trick to it. What he's calling out now? It's 'move forward.' But the bugle itself even sounds like its singing. *We're marching forward! And moving ahead!*"

It seemed to make sense. But did that apply to all of the bugle calls? Nearly every one, as I soon found out.

She anticipated the next one. "Trot. *Ta-Trot. Ta-Trot.* See? It's easy."

It still took me most of the morning to learn the drills.

Galloping, galloping, galloping boys! to speed us up.

To the left! would direct us to take a sharp left.

The fun part was what they called the "charge." I hardly expected such excitement.

Gallop boys with your sabers, with your sabers, for the charge!

The boys charged down the hillside, whooping and hollering all the way, though the captain of the company told them that they were not to yell like those "rotten Rebels."

After the charge we halted again and the men were ordered to sheathe their sabers and commence firing. The men pulled out their Sharps rifles (almost) in unison and began to fire. Unfortunately for them, many of the horses were not used to such a large amount of gunfire and leaped and plunged, some successfully removing their riders and fleeing back to the place where they had been previously tied.

The captain became infuriated and yelled orders, but to no avail. "Cease fire! To your horses! To your horses!" I became anxious but Ben's steady hand kept me in place.

Finally after nearly an hour had passed, the troops had rounded up their horses and were in line again. The captain sighed, disappointed. It was dinnertime, though, and so he commanded his troops to return the horses and prepare for lunch.

There were three drills that day, two of them mounted drills. It was an exciting time and I was learning a lot of new things about just how the cavalry unit worked, but I was weary by the end of the day. I stood beside the paint mare, who, as I learned, was named Catori.

We stood quietly eating hay while Ben put away saddles, bridles and other equipment. The captain sat nearby, talking with him.

"I can't believe that some of these boys don't know how to properly ride a horse!" he said, disgusted.

"Well, you have to think," Ben replied, "some of them live or have lived in cities. Many of them live in towns. They don't need to ride a horse every day."

"True," the captain answered. "But they're going to have to learn to ride and shoot. Fast. Real fast. How are they going to get away from the Bushwhackers or Rebs? And besides, I hear word that we're going to have to pack up and march out soon."

Ben raised an eyebrow, curious. "Really?" he asked simply.

"There's a large force of Rebs in Arkansas. If we can meet up with the Army of the Southwest before we get there and then join up with a larger force, we'd be able to take them."

Ben smiled. "That would be good. Perhaps the men will have something more to squash besides the bugs out of their hardtack.

Now please excuse me as I need to help the men gather some firewood."

"I have work to do as well," the captain said, and the two left.

I looked to the west, to the setting sun and sighed. "Do you think we're really going into battle?" I asked Catori.

"Possibly. It really depends on if we do meet up with the other brigade."

"Do you worry about it at all? I mean, I can imagine that it would be pretty crazy, even though I have never been in battle before."

She snorted. "Nah. It'll be fun."

I looked at her, obviously puzzled.

"Okay, it won't be all fun. But it will at least be exciting. The same routine of drills, marching and more drills is getting old. It will be nice to actually meet up with the enemy."

I looked upward to the sky, and wondered where Shiloh was or what he was doing. Perhaps he wasn't involved in any of this war yet. Maybe he had found a home with a family, or maybe he was lucky enough to stay with Casey.

Either way, I was not certain of his fate. But at this point, I was not sure of mine either.

Shiloh

The girl had enough sense not to attempt to get on my back but led me for a long time. I followed her and didn't attempt to get away or fight her at all.

When the sun was on the horizon, I could finally see her a little better. Her light blond braids shone in the sun, and her icy blues eyes were so determined. She was short, her head barely above my withers, and under her coat she wore a patched dress that barely went below her knees.

Near mid-morning we came to a clearing in the woods. I was surprised. The building ahead was merely a shack, with a tin roof over the top of it and barrels around to collect rainwater. Chickens wandered in the yard and a goat was by the porch. When she got near the house, three small humans ran outside to meet her.

"Sarah! Sarah!" they yelled, "where didja get that horse?"

A woman came outside after them, who I considered to be their mother. "Sarah!" she exclaimed with a scowl, then asked the same question, "Where did you get that horse?"

Sarah didn't seem to have a problem lying about it. "Mr. Robertson said he would pay me two dollars to break 'im in."

Her mother sighed. "It's not the best time to be takin' in a horse right now, even if you would make money training 'im."

"Oh, don't worry about it," Sarah countered, "I will feed 'im myself. There should be enough grass for 'im out back, for awhile anyway."

"I'm not worried about feeding 'im," her mother continued, but Sarah interrupted.

"And I would keep 'im away from Jack and Donnie so they wouldn't get hurt at all, and I'll keep up with all my chores, promise."

"Sarah!" her mother said loudly, "that's not what it's about." Sarah was quiet.

"Jack! Donnie! Git out back and feed the animals. I need to talk to Sarah; she'll show ya the horse later."

Sarah looked concerned. Her brothers ran in the house and her mother sat on the porch, where Sarah led me and then joined her mother.

"Sarah," her mother sighed, "I know it's hard with yer pa gone away but before he left we had talked about some things."

"What things?" Sarah asked nervously.

"Well," her mother started, "we've been thinkin' bout sending you to live with yer aunt and uncle in Charleston."

"But why?"

"You know your pa and I want something better for ya. Your Aunt Amelia lives on a plantation near there and you could get an education there—you could learn yer manners, learn to sew and cook better than I can teach ya. It would give ya a chance to get out of Vernon County and you could see so many more new and exciting things."

"But I don't want to!"

"Think about it, Sarah. I'm givin' ya an opportunity that I've never had before. Your pa and I just want what's best for ya. Why wouldn't ya want to go?"

"I don't want ta sit and rot," she replied, "learning some 'lady-like occupations.' There's so many more things to do. I want to help out with the cause!"

Her mother sighed again, exasperated. "What could *you* do to help the cause?"

"I don't know yet," Sarah said, excited. "I wanna go to war, like Jeremiah did. Maybe I could 'pprentice with a nurse. Maybe I could help feed the soldiers, or I could care for their horses. I'm good at that. Or maybe they would let me fight. 'Cuz I know how to shoot," she said, feigning to aim a gun across the yard.

Her mother gasped and stood up, grabbing her daughter's hand while she did. "Don't ya ever say that again! I've already lost two of my men, yer pa and yer brother to that 'war,' and who knows for sure if'n they're comin' back? Yer sixteen, for heaven's sake! You are going to your uncle and aunt's place, and that's final! You'd better get your things together, because I will be taking you to the train station, a week from today, mysalf."

Her mother threw Sarah's arm down and marched into the house, slamming the door behind her. Sarah stood speechless for a minute before she turned to me. "Ma just don't understand what the 'cause' is," she said, almost more to herself than to me. "It's the second great revolution—it's a fight for freedom! The North is bent on sending soldiers down here to invade our homeland, but Lincoln can't tell us what to do. And it says in the constitution that if'n our government becomes tyrannical it is our duty to conquer it and re-establish a new one, and so that's exactly what we are going to do. My pa went to war, and so did Jeremiah, so why can't I? Is it just because I'm a female?"

She led me to the corral in the back and started throwing hay in for me to eat, but kept talking. "And I don't know why I need any silly 'manners' or anything like that, either. That's stupid. I don't just wanna sit around and make clothes or cook fancy food."

She made her way around the backside of me, and crouched down beside my injured leg. "Ugh, that's bad," she said quietly. "Let's see what we can do." She grabbed the large splinter from my lower hind leg and with one quick motion pulled it completely out. I felt a searing pain and jumped backwards, but she was already out of the way. When I had settled down again, she pulled a rag out of her pocket and mopped up some of the blood. “It’s a miracle yer not lame,” she said softly, “I can’t believe you can still walk so well.” After she had finished cleaning the wound, she bandaged it tightly, talking to me the entire time to keep me calm. “In any event,” she continued, “Somethin’ exciting is brewing. I wanna be a part of it. I wanna join in the fight, before it’s over!”

She stopped here for a minute and stroked my shoulders. “That’s it. I’m goin’ whether my mother ‘lows it or not. I’m going to make history, and you’re coming with me!”

She had one week to make up her mind, anyhow. I didn’t know if she really was planning on running away from home and attempting to do something with the Confederate army or not. But whatever she did, she seemed pretty determined. I mean, hadn’t she already stolen me? That was already pretty un-ladylike. Sarah was stubborn, just like me. I think we would actually make a pretty good pair.

She began trying to train me the next day. She didn’t know where I was coming from, and so she started slow, the saddle blanket first, next she cinched up the saddle and stepped back. I stood still for a while but then exploded, the memory of the last time this happened still in my mind. I kicked dust and leaves into the air in a wild fury, my eyes rolling white in fear. She sat quietly by the fence, watching me blow off all my steam until I finally stopped and stood, sweaty, tired, and breathing loudly.

“Thata boy,” she said quietly. “That’s all I need from you now.” And to my surprise, she pulled off the saddle and saddle blankets, carefully making sure not to let the stirrups or any other part of the saddle hit against my sides. She scratched behind my ears gently, then left.

I watched after her curiously. I was happy that she was breaking me in slowly, not trying to beat me into submission as the last man had done, but I still distrusted any human that tried to ride on my back.

I knew her plan was to break me in before the week was up, though. I didn't know quite how she did it, but in three days she was on my back, directing me with the long leather reins connected to the bit in my mouth. She truly was good at working with horses, but it was because I trusted her, and with her I felt like it was more of a team effort instead of a master and the submissive beast.

I knew now that it was only a matter of time before she decided to leave home. As she had said, it was now or never.

I was right. A few days later she came outside to the small corral. I heard her feet crunching on the leaves before I saw her. There was only a sliver of a golden moon outside, and so darkness cloaked the area like a blanket of blackness. She was wearing her too-short dress with pants and boots underneath. She had the saddle and blanket, bridle and a canvas bag full of supplies that she would need for the journey.

"Are you ready, Shiloh?" she asked quietly, "because I'm not sure if I am." She threw the saddle over my back. I willingly accepted the bit into my mouth as she silently pulled the bridle over my ears. My wound was mostly healed by now; the bandage was still wrapped around my hind foot but I was able to walk and bear weight on it. She led me outside of the corral and climbed aboard, kicking me into a frenzied gallop.

We flew away from the little shack, my hooves pounding hard on the cold ground as Sarah leaned in closer to avoid being whipped in the face by the long tree branches that seemed to lean in, attempting to grab her and pull her from the saddle.

She was braver than I was, but it was her bravery that kept me going. *Ba da rump, ba da rump.* My hooves kept up the rhythm, but my smooth gait made it feel as if we were sailing across the hard ground.

After a good amount of running, she pulled the reins in to slow me down. I gave in a little at a time, until we were finally walking along the little trail through the woods. I was out of breath, breathing heavily in the silent darkness. She scratched along the side of my sweaty neck.

"Good boy," she said, "it's not too far from here. I know where they are setting up to accept volunteers for the Confederacy. We just have to keep on this trail for a few more hours."

She was right. Later, after the sun had risen, we took a sharp right onto another little trail, through some more thick woods until we could see a clearing in the distance, down below in a valley.

Sure enough, there was a large group of organized men and horses. We had made it. She dismounted and put a hand on my shoulder. "Looks good, huh Shiloh? We finally made it! It's going ta be so exciting. I wanna work with the hosses, but maybe they'll let me be a nurse's assistant or somethin' like dat. Maybe I'll get to see Pa or Jerimiah! I ain't sure. I don't know 'zactly what they let ladies do to help. But, in any event, I need ta get out of these britches. I know they're not ladylike."

She removed the britches from under her dress and straightened her unruly hair, then smoothed her wrinkled dress. She packed the things into her canvas bag and then climbed on and kicked me into a lope, down to the clearing below. Before she got there she slowed me to a walk into the group of men. There were a few off-colored white canvas tents and men all around, a large group of horses were tethered in the trees in the distance.

Sarah dismounted and watched the scene before her for a moment before she stopped a man who walked in front of her, hardly taking any notice.

“’Scuse me,” she said, “I’m lookin’ for Lieutenant Sawyers, please.”

The man pointed. “Right over there. He’s a busy man though so you may have to wait awhile to speak to him.”

She nodded. “Thank you.”

She led me over to where the Lieutenant Sawyers stood, a great man in a light grayish uniform who had a bushy brown hair and long brown beard. He stood beside another man who was sitting at a table filling out paperwork while talking to the Lieutenant Sawyers. Sarah waited for a break in the conversation before she broke in.

“Excuse me?” She asked nervously.

Both of the men turned to look at her, surprised. “Can I help you?”

Sarah straightened up. “My name is Sarah Cooper. I’m lookin’ to volunteer. I’ll do whatever you need me to. I can apprentice as a nurse, I can take care of hosses, or cook food and help clean up camp.”

The men looked at each other, then turned to her. They burst out laughing. “What are you, girl, like twelve years old? How can you help? This is a man’s war. Even if you could, the battlefield’s no place for a young girl.”

The man filling out paperwork laughed so hard that he needed to wipe tears from his eyes. Lieutenant Sawyers howled with laughter; he was an intimidating man but to see him laugh in such a way was almost comical in itself. Sarah’s face turned bright red in embarrassment as the two laughing men made such a scene that the men attending to other duties around them stopped and looked over as they passed by.

“I ain’t twelve! I’m sixteen for Pete’s sake, and I can be a lot of help if’n I set my mind to it! I mean, look at this ‘ere horse, for example. I stole ‘im myself, right out of Yankee hands.”

The Lieutenant stopped laughing for a moment, swallowing for air before he took a better look at Sarah and me. “Wait a minute,” he said, “aren’t you James Cooper’s girl? What are ya doing out here?”

“I told ya—” she started.

“Don’t you worry your pretty little mind none,” he said, “I’ve got someone who will bring you right back.

“Briggs!” he yelled to a man, who began walking toward us.

“Besides,” the Lieutenant continued, “as far as I’m concerned you’ve already helped out the Confederate cause more than you’ve needed to.”

Sarah opened her mouth, but shut it again and said nothing, looking utterly upset and confused.

“This horse would make a good addition to our cavalry unit. Hand him over to this gentleman and Briggs will make sure to get you home.”

Suddenly Sarah understood as the man reached for the reins. She looked from Sawyers, to the man gesturing for her to surrender her horse, and back at me before she exploded.

“You ain’t takin’ my horse!” she yelled, and jumped on my back in a split second and turned my head around, kicking me into a gallop.

The men behind stood in shock for a minute, before I heard the Lieutenant call out, “aboard your horses! Chase that horse down, make sure the girl gets home.”

We were up for quite the chase. The warm mid-morning sun warmed me more than I thought necessary. Sweat poured down my back and my sore foot began to throb as the bandaging came loose in the wild gallop uphill. I wasn’t sure that we would make it, I had been traveling all night and I knew that I wasn’t the fastest horse out there in the first place.

Even though hot tears ran down Sarah’s face, her enthusiasm to get away spurred me on. She was determined. I heard the horses' feet behind me, and I leaped forward in another burst of speed. As we came closer to the forested area, tree branches whipped her face and my sides but still she pushed me forward. The men behind in gray uniforms had taller, stronger horses, but she knew the two of us had a stronger will.

I leaped over fallen branches in my path, nearly throwing Sarah from the saddle, but she grabbed onto my mane and pulled herself up. I could hear them getting closer. I made a quick turn to the left, around a large rock and suddenly attempted to stop.

There was a steep cliff on the other side, sharply declining into the riverbed below. But it was too late to stop. I squealed, then fell backward onto my rump and slid down the hill, Sarah determinedly holding onto the reins, with my mane wrapped through her fingers.

The horses behind us were able to stop in time and the men's faces held great surprise as they watched the commotion. It was probably the only bit of excitement they had in awhile, to see the young girl sliding down the hill on the little gray horse, loose pebbles and dust flying up around us.

I continued to slide downwards, until the decline stopped and led into the river, where I fell onto my knees and frantically stood up, the shanks of the bit slapping against the reins as I turned my head every which way in order to figure out what we should do.

But for Sarah, there was only one thing we could do, and that was move forward. She kicked me forward into the cold river and I had no choice but to swim. The current rushed around my figure and soaked Sarah's dress, drenching myself and the saddle in muddy water as we went. I paddled through the water until I finally reached the other side of the river, exhausted, and climbed up the bank.

Sarah sighed, tired as well, but turned around to see if the men were following. We saw them standing up on the other side, scratching their heads in sheer disbelief. There was even a sparkle of laughter in their horses' eyes as they watched our great escapade as well. They stood there for a while longer, until they gave up and turned their horses, heading back to the camp.

Sarah dismounted, her dress covered in mud and her hair soaked. I shook violently to rid myself of the cold water, and she wrung the bottom of her dress out. *What now?* I wondered. Would she go back home after all of that?

She adjusted the saddle. "We're not going back," she said, as if reading my mind. "We need to keep going forward in case they send someone else after us. But I'm certain that I'm not going back home so ma can send me Charleston." She was shaking now, more out of frustration than from the cold. She opened the canvas pack and pulled out her brother's knife that she had brought along and unsheathed it.

"No. There's only one way I'm going to be able to do this," she said more to herself than me. And with that, she cut through first one white-blond braid, then the other. She laid both on the ground beside her canvas pack, put on her trousers and an oversized shirt, and made her way to the river to see if she could possibly be able to see her reflection.

I stood tiredly and watched her as she crouched down by the riverside, attempting to straighten her hair into a more masculine look. She stood up and turned to face me, and I was surprised at how different she actually looked. Maybe she didn't look exactly like a man, but she didn't look like the same little girl anymore. With her blond hair cut short, her dirty face helped make her look like any little Reb boy.

She turned back and washed the last remnants of tears from her face, and grabbed the long split reins. "Let's go, Shiloh." She looked up to the sun hanging low in the west. "I'm so tired, I wish that we could stop and rest for a while, but we really need to move on." Sarah grabbed the two braids that she had left by the river bank and moved to put them into her pack, but stopped suddenly and frowned.

"I won't need these, and I don't want to get caught with them." And with that, she tossed both braids into the river water. She pulled the reins and walked beside me, and we set off once again into the woods.

We walked and walked, following the river, until the sun had set and risen once again. We had seen no sign of human life for miles, and we were both exhausted. During the midmorning, Sarah and I found a clearing, and it was here that she hobbled my hind legs so that I wouldn't stray too far away and collapsed on the ground, exhausted. She slept curled in a little ball for several hours, I didn't go too far away but grazed at a few patches of grass while she slept. When she awoke, she blinked hard in the late-day sun, slowly rising up from the hard ground with her short blond hair sticking out in all directions.

I turned to look at her, as if asking "now what?"

She stretched and scratched her head, then stood up. "I've got another plan," she said to me. I listened, intrigued with what this spunky girl would do now. "I've heard talk about another regiment. It's more to the west, but I'm sure that they have never heard of my father or brother before, and I do look more like a boy now. Maybe they'll take me in as a regular since everyone seems to think I'm too much of a little girl to be any help."

This girl was crazy. I had never seen such a female in my life, she acted so differently than any of the ones I had seen before. But I liked her spirit, and so I was determined to go with her wherever she went.

We continued to travel, most of the time she walked beside me to conserve my energy and to keep herself awake. We traveled for days until we finally found an army of men. We stayed hidden in the trees at first, to get a better look at them. This camp was even larger than the one before, with hundreds of men at work, drilling, or milling about and lines of horses picketed. Sarah squinted her eyes a little bit. "Yup," she said, "'dem are definitely Confederates. Look at all that gray! Besides, I can always tell a Reb when I see one!"

"Now it's time to see how well I can impersonate a boy." She put a hand on my shoulder. "One more time," Sarah said, looking into the army ahead of us. "Now's my chance."

Tucker

We marched forward for days. Finally we had come to an area where we met a larger gathering of men that formed what was to be called the Union Army of the Southwest. I don't think that I had ever seen so many people organized in one place. There were men from several different regiments and places—from Iowa, from Illinois, Indiana, and my home state of Missouri. There were a few other cavalry units, there were battery and regiment upon regiment full of infantry. It made me nervous but stirred up Catori."We're finally getting ready to face the enemy," Catori announced to me. "Aren't you excited?"

Excited for what? All we were doing was marching, then camping, then getting up early and marching again. The weather was becoming bitterly cold as the new year came and went .The men complained of sore legs and muscles and horses balked with saddle sores and lameness.

Soon after we had set up camp one late afternoon, I overheard a conversation between the captain and Ben.

"Keep those horses well-fed, we're going to need them. We are close to where the Rebs are camped," the Captain was saying as I saw him walking from around the tents and toward where the horses were kept.

I heard Ben's voice answer back. "Will do. You've heard word from the scouts?"

"Yes sir. Arnold says their camp has been spotted in Benton County."

Ben sighed. "It's best we be ready then, I suppose." The captain left, and Ben came over to give the horses more grain.

He carried the heavy bag of feed like it was nothing, scooping grain into the horses' feed buckets. The horses snapped at the food hungrily, gulping whatever they could get while some even attempted to snatch it from the others.

"Come now, ey," Ben told them quietly in his soft Irish-sounding accent. "Eat your own food."

After all of the horses had been fed, Ben put up the food and then made himself comfortable sitting up against a thick tree trunk. He looked up to the horses again, as if to make a quick double-check that they were okay, and then opened a little case beside him. He pulled out paper, pen and a hard surface to write on. He looked thoughtful for a moment, then began scratching onto the paper.

I had finished my grain, and looked to him, confused about what he was doing. Catori was tethered farther away so I couldn't ask her about the strange ways of the humans. I nickered to him.

Ben looked up. "Finished?" he asked. I still looked at him, and he smiled. "I'm just writing a letter, to my sister up north actually. She was pretty upset when I left. I hope she's doing alright. I like to at least write and let 'em know that I'm doing okay." He continued writing until the sun had nearly set. He said that he liked to write away from the camp, since it was quieter and the sound of the horses munching contentedly on their hay seemed to calm him.

Soon he had finally finished and lifted his letter closer to read it.

Dear Amelia, he read aloud, to check himself for errors. *It has been quite a time since I last had an opportunity to write to you, but I will take the present opportunity to let you know that I am yet among the living, and I cannot wait to return home to you and the rest of the family.*

In fact, my present time is engaged mainly in simple and lonely tasks, such as those of collecting firewood, caring for the horses, digging or building fortifications, and other camp duties. We have also been spending a fair amount of time marching, in an attempt to locate the enemy, who have been doing an excellent job of skirting our every attempt.

We have been getting closer though, and rumors going through the camp tell that we may be in battle with them soon. Sending all of my love to you and the rest of the family.
Sincerely your brother,
Pvt. Benjamin Roth

He looked up from the letter and at me, nodding his head. "There's not much to tell 'er, but what there is I've tried to explain a little bit. Living as an enlisted man isn't quite as much fun as I thought it would be. We have yet to get into a real battle, too.

"We haven't had any casualties yet in our regiment. Other than the few men that have gotten sick—measles, dropsy, dysentery or the fever—there's been no battle-related wounds or deaths. But we might be coming close to changing that."

He was right. We were getting closer to the Rebs every single day. I had heard talk of these "Rebs," mostly from Catori, but also from the other horses and from what I overheard from the soldiers. But I had yet to actually see what enemy we were facing.

A tall gray horse, called Captain, was helpful to me in explaining a lot about what was going on. I talked about the details of what was going on with him late into the night when he was tethered next to me. He told me a lot of the same things that Catori told me, it only seemed that he had a little more experience behind it. His master was a colonel, leader of the fourth Missouri if I remember right. Captain had seen battle before; he knew what it was like. He would often recite the tales of his experiences in the battles and skirmishes. At first they were exciting, but after awhile, they grew tiresome. "Uh-huh," I would answer as he told me a story of the same battle for the second or third time. "Sounds like it would be terrible."

"You have no idea," he answered. "Like most of the horses here, you're still green."

"Green?" I echoed. "I would say not! I've been trained in, and I haven't bucked since the day they put the saddle on me."

He laughed. "Na, I'm referencing green in the way that most of the soldiers around here reference it. You've never seen the elephant before."

"Seen the elephant?" I asked again, confused.

"Battle," he said somberly.

I thought about it for awhile. The elephant couldn't be too bad.

We trudged on, until we reached somewhere in Benton County, where we were able to stop near a place on Sugar Creek. "They'll probably dig a few trenches here near the creek where it will make a good fortification," Catori explained to me. "Then we wait for the Rebs to come. We've spent this long getting them out of Missouri, this is our last chance to push them all the way back to southern Arkansas."

The brigade general Samuel Curtis decided to stop where we were for a few different reasons. He could stop here to wait for reinforcements and for his long line of supply wagons. The spot also offered a shelter and water, and so we hunkered down and waited for a rebel attack from the south. The horses were picketed behind the main line, where Ben along with most of the other soldiers began the tedious job of digging trenches. With shovels constantly digging into the ground, there was hardly time for more than basic care of the equines in the camp. Occasionally Ben or others would come out to ride the horses to give us exercise as well as scout the area, but other than that, we stood picketed most of the time.

Soon, however, word was brought to Curtis about the advancing Confederates from the scouts as well as Unionists who lived in Arkansas. Curtis sent out a cavalry unit and I was lucky enough to go along.

Ben saddled me up and the other men did the same with their horses, and then he mounted gracefully, kicking his blunt spurs into my sides to get me moving. I jumped forward into a lope ahead of the others, and Ben curled the reins in his fingers, urging me to slow the pace a little. We trotted along the old Wire Road, the horses' breath fogging in the chilly morning air and the sounds of jangling bits and spurs lit up the atmosphere with excitement. I couldn't wait to see what our enemies truly looked like, or what battle would be like. But as I sensed the conflict coming closer, my stomach started to get fluttery. I didn't know what we were getting ourselves into, but there was no turning back now.

We scouted around the area for much of the day, having no luck. But for each unknown noise or twig that snapped in the wrong direction, the men nervously glanced around themselves. The Confederates could be anywhere, and for many of the soldiers, this was their first time in battle.

Much of the day was spent quietly riding around the area. Ben led me near the front of the group of about a dozen men on horseback, but I yawned hugely as we traveled. There was nothing going on.

Suddenly the officer in front of us pulled his horse to a stop. The rest of the troops behind him halted, wondering what had made him stop.

"What is it?" Ben asked the officer.

"Shhh!" He replied sharply, and pointed through the trees downhill.

Down below there were men walking through the woods, noisily talking amongst themselves. Most of them were in butternut gray cotton uniforms, while others wore canvas pants and cotton or flannel shirts. A lot of them wore wide-brimmed hats to protect them from the sun, and most of the older ones had long beards. My ears pricked forward in their direction. Well, we had gotten a look at them. Could we go now?

The general pinpointed their direction below the bluff, then turned his horse, hoping to get back to the Union forces without the Rebs noticing us.

We walked away quietly for a few moments, until the horses were kicked into a faster speed, and we galloped back to the entrenchments.

When we got there, the general of our little unit wanted to talk to Curtis.

"We've found the Rebs, and they're not more than a few miles away. They're heading toward the right flank."

Men raced into position, getting ready for the attack. Curtis calmed them and began to give orders. When the two sides did meet, he wanted his soldiers to be as orderly as possible. Curtis ordered the leader of the cavalry, general Bussey, to march forward and meet the Rebs on the Ford Road.

"We'll buy ourselves some time," he said, pointing at a map of the area, while talking to the commander of the cavalry.

"If our scouts are correct, Van Dorn's troops were coming around Pea Ridge on both sides. I'll be sure to send some of the infantry to meet them at Elkhorn, but it looks as if a large group is heading over on Ford Road now. If the mounted infantry can meet them there and buy us some time, we should be able to organize our infantry and whip these Rebs. This is our chance to make sure that the Union holds control of Missouri and Arkansas."

General Bussey nodded slowly, his dark eyes scanning the map below. It may be risky, but surely if he could hold them off the Union soldiers would be able to win in the end. He understood what Curtis wanted to do, and so he mounted up on his tall black horse and ordered the third Iowa cavalry regiment as well as our regiment to do the same. We trotted away, intent on completing our mission.

I could sense Ben's uneasiness as we trotted down the bluff and through the wooded area. He didn't know what was coming, but at least we knew more than the gray-clad men that we attacked.

I was kind of disappointed that we didn't get to hear the harsh "Rebel yell" that Captain had told me about. When we got closer to the pack of Rebs, the men got prepared for the attack. The soldiers pulled out their rifles and pistols. Tension hung in the air thicker than fog.

For my first battle, I didn't know what to expect. The morning was still a little cool and windy, since it was only March, but the heat of day would fall upon us later as the battle did. The trees had yet to grow any leaves on them, but the grass had started to turn green already, and my head had been yanked up more than a couple times when I tried to eat from the lush grass growing beneath my feet.

Bussey lined us up in the way that he wanted us, and we prepared to charge. He had to go about the charge in just the right way.

"We are mounted infantry, men," he told them. "But don't feel like you need to dismount and shoot right away. Flee if you have to. Our only objective is to distract, not to obliterate."

The men agreed. They pointed their weapons forward and brought their horses into a lope, ready to charge. The Rebs already had a bit of a clue what was going on and were prepared to meet.

The clash was not what I expected, though, and throughout the two-day battle, it would only get worse. The Union cavalry smashed into the Confederate line, brandishing their weapons. The Rebs seemed confused at first. Their line scattered before it became straight again. Bussey kept us as straight as possible before we hit the Southern forces.

Captain and Catori had told me before that tactics were changing in this war. In wars previous the cavalry was an important part of the battlefield, and a man on a horse had a distinct advantage over soldiers on foot. Yet this war was different. The cavalry was hardly ever used in direct combat; the mounted infantry was sometimes. Rather, the cavalry and mounted infantry were used to deliver messages or scout areas, or sometimes to provide a distraction, such as we were doing here.

But it hardly seemed less than direct combat at the time.

Men on both sides yelled, and bullets whizzed by us. Sometimes I could feel them going over the tops of my ears, but surprisingly they always missed Ben and me.

My skin flinched under the dangerous fire and I fought the urge to buck and run away from the fire. But Ben held me with a steady hand. He knew how to deal with horses, how to get them to trust him. With one hand he held the reins and in the other he held his pistol, shots ringing out when he was able to shoot, kicking me to cover when he knew that he couldn't. Many of the men dismounted to fire but Ben was a good shot from the saddle, and so he stayed there.

I was glad that the southern artillery wasn't here yet. From what I heard from Captain and Catori, the roar of the cannons is what frightened horses the most, and for good reason. Captain relayed stories of horses getting their legs blown off by the cannon balls, or men ripped in half from the force of the huge rolling ball of fire.

I shivered again. The battle was just beginning but it already sounded terrible. The sound of screaming horses, the pop of muskets and pistols, and the beginnings of a Rebel yell were heard throughout the woods and along the road where we fought. Occasionally I could see a burst of flame from the men's rifles as they stopped to fire. Men and horses stumbled in confusion as they struggled to keep the lines straight. I saw a few men fall, some of the wounded men crawling to take shelter from the battle while others stayed where they fell, blood soaking from their wounds into their uniforms and clothing.

Worriedly I looked around. I didn't see Catori or Captain anywhere. I didn't have too much time to worry about it though. I received commands from Ben but I tried to anticipate where he would want me to go next before he asked me to. He already had a lot to worry about.

After a few minutes that seemed like hours, I saw Catori rushing forward from behind us with a Union soldier on her back, the covered stirrups pounding against her sides as the man pushed her forward.

She and the soldier rushed to Bussey, who turned when he saw them. I saw the man on Catori's back lean forward to yell something into Bussey's ear. It must be the signal. The rest of the Union soldiers would be arriving soon.

I was right.

Soon after, I saw infantry regiments coming over the hill. It brought relief to the cavalry and mounted infantry units, who slowed and then burst forward with a renewed assurance, lines and lines of infantry behind them. The confused Confederates scattered, but didn't cool down their valor in the heat of battle.

Though we had better odds now, the Federal troops were still being worn down, the dead and dying beginning to fill the battlefield. When the battle cleared out in some areas, carts were filled with wounded men, who were carried to the Elkhorn

Tavern. There they would receive amputations and care for their wounds.

Another horse slammed me from the side, and I fell to the ground. Ben fell a few feet from me, but quickly got up and returned fire. I stood to my feet and spun, ready to get out of the battlefield, but I was too late. Ben had already grabbed the reins and was determined to keep me there with him.

We fought all day until dusk, with no real result from the battle. When night came, both sides retreated to their campsites. It had been a hard-fought battle, and there were no clear winners on either side. The soldiers bedded down and prepared for a long night, even with the occasional *pops* of rifles still going on around them and the screams of the wounded that could be heard once one got closer to the Elkhorn Tavern. Ben tied me close to the other horses that were picketed and took his turn at watch, exhausted.

"It's not like I could sleep, anyway," he told me before he left for his duties. "Not after what I've seen today. But I have a feeling that it's going to be even worse tomorrow."

Shiloh

Sarah climbed onto my back and kicked me into a lope, and we emerged from the thick forest into the clearing. She and I both wondered what exactly was ahead of us, but we hoped that it would be better than what we had found at the last place.

"By the looks of this, it's a volunteer regiment. We should be able to get in somehow," she said to me as we loped along, her gaze never leaving the site in front of her.

We trotted into the camp, then slowed down to a walk. Sarah held her breath as she walked through the rows of men and tents, wondering if they would believe that she actually was a boy.

Many of the men who walked by wore the standard butternut gray uniforms, with wide-brimmed hats to shade their eyes from the sun. A lot of them worked to gather firewood or supplies, but many also spent some leisure time playing cards or using wide trees for target practice. There was a long line of horses picketed toward the west of the campsite, contentedly munching on hay or grass in the sun, their hind legs cocked to rest and their tails swishing flies away.

We soon enough found someone who appeared to be somewhat in charge. Sarah dismounted and looked up at him, removing her hat. "Hullo," she said cautiously. "My name is Sam West. I've bin lookin' to join a Confederate regiment somewhere where my services would be helpful. Cavalry preferably."

The man looked down at her, squinting his eyes from the sun. "Nice to meet you Mr. West. We are looking for help wherever we can get it. How old might you be?"

Sarah thought for a moment, before she answered, "Seventeen."

"What are yer parents names, and have they given consent for you to fight?"

"I have no parents," she answered, looking down. "I've bin on my own since I was fourteen, raised the youngins' up for a few years, but I left 'em with my aunt and uncle in Arkansas. I've been doing pretty good on my own but I want somethin' steady to keep me occupied."

The man raised his eyebrows. I wondered if he was going to believe it, but the way Sarah had said it sounded convincing enough.

"Sounds alright. We've got a place for you in here somewhere, though I doubt it's in the cavalry. Is that yer horse?"

"Yessir," she replied, "stole 'im outta Yankee hands myself."

He looked impressed. "Well, since most of our cavalry unit is made up of those men who have their own horses, we might have a spot for you there. Otherwise we'll have to put you somewhere in the infantry, Sam.

"Picket yer horse with the others, and we'll find a place for you." He smiled, appearing kind, and so Sarah smiled too as she turned and trotted away.

Later that night, the campsite was lit up with bonfires, and though they were supposed to be sleeping, many of the men lay awake talking with each other. The cool air of spring had died off and it began to get colder, and though I spent much of the day dozing, now that it was night, I shuffled restlessly among the other horses.

Sarah had found a spot in the "cavalry," or whatever it was that made up the cavalry in this unit. She slept on the ground close to where the horses were picketed, so close, that I could even hear some of their conversation.

I was glad to hear that it seemed like Sarah had even made some friends within the regiment. And we were far enough away from where she lived that it seemed that no one knew who she was, and she was disguised so well that maybe even those who knew her wouldn't recognize her.

She was on her stomach, but her head rested on her hands as she listened with fascination to an older man talk about what he had seen of the war so far.

"I 'member the first time I seen the Elephant," he was saying to her and the other boys that were around.

"The Elephant?" many of them asked, confused.

"That's what they call the first time men see battle," he said with a smirk. "You'll see. I won't be the only one that gets to brag about seein' the beast. And it's then that ya'll be able to prove yourself—yer courage. It's when you'll be able to prove yerself as a man to everyone else or as a yeller-belly, like some of these fools that have run off at the first sound of the artillery. You'll prove to all the men around you, and for your Confederate women back home, that yer a true man."

I saw Sarah hold back a little bit of a snicker. She dared not let it out, lest she be suspected of anything. She was already walking on thin ice.

"And maybe if yer lucky enuf," the man continued, "you'll be able to bring your own badge of courage home."

The boys around him looked curious, and so he took the opportunity to show off. "Like mine," he said, before pulling up his shirt sleeve to reveal a giant scar that extended from the bottom of his wrist all the way down to his elbow, still bright red.

"This is what I got up at Manassas. A blasting pile of shrapnel from those Feds got me, and ripped my arm to shreds. I believe that the doctors wanted to amputate it, but I wouldn't let 'em." The boys around him gasped in awe. They wanted to see the Elephant, too. Maybe get their own badge to bring home as proof that they had been in battle.

"Though I'm not sure if we're going to see battle here," the man kept on, "we ain't close to any Yankees yet. Yup, I can tell we've got a lot of marchin' yet until we get to the larger division. But in the meantime—we might be able to put our cavalry to the test yet."

The boys looked at him, confused again, and so he explained. "We might be able to go on a few raids."

Sarah and the other boys smiled. This sounded like a lot of fun after all.

———

This Confederate regiment of volunteer cavalry wasn't so bad. Almost all of the men who made up the regiment had brought their own horses, and it seemed like many of them (the men and the horses) knew each other pretty well. All of the men and boys were rough outdoorsman or farmers, they knew how to ride a horse and how to shoot a gun. There wasn't much need for drill practice, like in a Union cavalry, because these men already worked together well.

On paper, the cavalry regiments were supposed to have been made up of "troops" made up of up to a hundred men, and then ten troops made up a regiment. It wasn't even half-true for our cavalry. Ours was made up of a gang of about forty men, with an assortment of horses ranging from plow horses to thoroughbreds. For now, we resided with a few other regiments of infantry and artillery and would march to a larger group of men that needed us. From what I had heard, we were going to be heading east in order to try to find the Army of the Mississippi, led by Beauregard.

We were still a lot of miles away though, and so it would probably take us awhile to get there. We had to march almost every day at first, and that wasn't much fun. Some of the men tried to make it more interesting, singing out early Confederate anthems in the brisk March air:

We are a band of brothers,
And native to the soil,
Fighting for the property
We gained by honest toil;
And when our rights were threatened,
The cry rose near and far,
"Hurrah for the Bonnie Blue Flag
That bears a single star!

As long as the Union
Was faithful to her trust,
Like friends and like brothers,
Both were kind and just,
But now, when Northern treachery
Attempts our rights to mar,
We hoist on high the Bonnie Blue Flag
That bears a single star

Hurrah! Hurrah!
For Southern Rights Hurrah!
Hurrah for the Bonnie Blue Flag
That bears a single star!

The men got tired of singing, soon enough, after the skies opened up and decided to drench the soldiers in a heavy downpour. At the first few slips and falls the men laughed but soon after they ceased as they found it wasn't quite so funny. The rain drenched the men and weighed them down, it soaked the horses and gave them saddle sores. The repeated falling into the mud didn't even draw a glance now as the men became used to the constant fight against the slippery sludge. The rain froze men to the bone. It was more of a burden than a laugh to them now.

We kept on marching for a few days, meeting up and joining a few other regiments but not getting much closer to our Army of the Mississippi.

One night as the men rested from their marching, I sat dozing peacefully with the other horses that were picketed outside of where the men camped.

I was munching on a few bits of hay quietly, when I suddenly saw a figure move from behind the trees. I looked over to where the men were camping and saw the tent flap fly upwards, a man or two stick their heads out of the opening, and glance around cautiously before sneaking outside of it. Quick as a fox and as silent as a Sunday morning church service, Sarah made her way to my side.

She picked up the heavy saddle and threw it over my back, and began tightening the cinches. I saw other men do the same with their horses. Sarah silently picked up her carbine and slid it into the scabbard while I watched her with interest.

I saw another boy who was perhaps even younger than she move close to her side. "Do you know what's goin' on, Sam?" he asked timidly.

"Raid," Sarah whispered. "There's a small Yankee supply train comin' through a couple miles east. If'n we can head over there in time we can cut off some of their supplies they'll be needin'."

He nodded in acknowledgement, and moved to his mount. All of the men worked quickly. When she was finished, Sarah stuck her foot in the stirrup and hopped into the saddle, pulling me back with both hands on the reins before I could take off.

When the other men were prepared to go, we galloped off. I was ready to run. I stretched out my legs and pushed forward, though Sarah had to continuously pull back on the reins to keep me in a slower gallop with the rest of the group.

We emerged from the forest, ran down a bluff and into some prairie land, and then loped on for a few miles until we reached what looked like a campsite. There was a dying fire and a few tents, with parked wagons and picketed horses around the fire. We found a place to hide, and then Jerry, the oldest and most experienced of the men in the cavalry, directed us to what we should do.

"I'd like to take everythin'," he was saying to the group, "but with as small a force as we've got here, I ain't sure it'll be possible."

His dark eyes scanned the scene in front of him from beneath brown bushy eyebrows as he scratched his beard. "Since we all know that one good Southern boy can whup ten or more o' those Yankees, I'm thinkin' we'll fare alright."

I grew jittery as he continued on, explaining what we would take, what we would destroy, and so on. I nodded my head, jangling the metal pieces of the bridle until Sarah yanked hard on those reins one last time.

"So are we ready, boys?" Jerry asked, a glint in his eye.

"Yessir!" they replied.

With that, he turned his horse and led the way, letting out a piercing Rebel scream that would turn any Yankee into pudding upon hearing it. The others followed suit, whooping and hollering while they pulled their guns out of their scabbards.

We charged toward them. The Yankees were in complete surprise, and they woke up to what they probably wished was a nightmare. They came out of their tents, out from under the wagons, from inside the wagons in complete surprise, but pulled out their guns as quickly as they could and began to fire.

Sarah and I dodged the hailing bullets that bombarded us and ricocheted off random objects to blast toward us. The Yankees were in complete confusion, but the Rebs were only slightly more organized.

Men were yelling and running in all directions, horses were colliding into objects and people, and the gunshots seemed to forever be ringing in my ears. I fought the urge to shy at every little thing and forced my body to be in sync with Sarah's hurried commands. Her usually steady hands seemed to shake a little at the threat of the bullets; I could feel the tiny vibrations through the reins to the bit in my mouth. But I knew that I had to be as strong as she was. I charged forward and Sarah dropped the reins, trusting me to hold steady while she brought her gun to her shoulder to shoot.

She didn't have to. As she rode up closer to the men in the moonlight, other members of the cavalry, including Jerry, surrounded the group of Yankees that were left. The cowards dropped their weapons on the ground with a barely-heard *thud* while they put their hands into the air. I raised my head as Sarah put her gun down, the look of fear on her face replaced with a scowl of disgust. The Yankees stood in front of us, many of them were as old or slightly older than Sarah, their hair tousled, some in their sleeping clothes yet; their dirty white faces glimmering with sweat in the hot night air.

Jerry rode closer to them. "That's right ya darn Yanks," he spat, "you ain't got much of a chance when you know one Reb is worth ten a yer souls." If he remembered the slight bit of doubt that he had before the raid, he completely cloaked it now, a look of confidence over his face.

"Wha…What are you going to do with us?" one of the Yankees stuttered.

He turned his horse away. "Hmmm…." he replied, "I don't know yet. Let the rest of my men take inventory of your supplies. That's all I'm really after anyway. Then afterward we'll decide what to do with you power-hungry young Yanks. I'm sure there's a prison camp somewhere south of here that will take ya. They need more white-colored 'hanging' decorations," he said with a laugh, many of the others joining in.

Many of the Yankee men's faces fell at the discouraging fate that was facing them. I shuddered at the thought. Many of the Southern men felt so vindictive, resenting even the sight of a Yankee soldier. But the worst of the Southern revenge I had yet to see.

Many of the men stayed near the small group of Yankees that were left, keeping their carbines and sharps pointed at them. Sarah turned me and trotted off to see what kind of spoils the small cavalry had earned themselves.

We found men loading up wagons and harnessing horses and mules in the darkness. "We need people to drive wagons," one of them was saying.

"I can do it," Sarah spoke up, I'll tie Shiloh to the back of the wagon bed, he'll be alright."

"Aright," the man answered. "I need ya to help some of the men finish packing up and hitching mules." Sarah nodded in answer and turned me softly away to tie my bridle to the wagon bed.

When the men had finished taking their spoils, the Yankee men stood anxiously awaiting orders. Jerry rode up to the group of about a dozen men.

"Well, I've decided to go easy on ya, seeings' how none of ya are even in a real regiment. You've been aiding the enemy, and dat's worthy of bein' hanged. But I've decided to let ya'll go."

A few quiet sighs of relief could be heard from the Yankees.

“But don’t think I’ll let ya off easy,” Jerry barked. I was able to barely see his face in the breaking dawn of day if I turned my head from the back board of the wagon I was tied to. He seemed so much calmer and collected when he was talking to his men compared to the way he growled at these Yankees.

“I’m going to take everything you have, everything that you were personally delivering to those agents of Satan. But dat probably won’t teach ya’ll the lesson that I need it to.”

As Jerry sat on his horse, he pulled out his rifle with one hand and pointed it casually at the men.

“You have two minutes to pull everything out of yer pockets,” he told them.

The Yankees looked at each other, confused. Jerry’s rifle and a couple others clicked. “I mean it.”

The Yankees pulled everything out of their pockets, from knifes and cards to pictures and small packages of gunpowder, letting everything drop to the ground.

“Good,” Jerry said quietly with his gun still on the Yankees. “Now strip. I want everything but your nightclothes, from those of you who are dressed.”

I watched disgustedly as the men pulled off their clothes, jackets, pants, whatever covered them until they were in their undergarments, completely embarrassed.

Jerry motioned to a couple of the younger men, who moved to pick up the clothes and other articles off the ground.

“Let that be a lesson to ya,” he said. “You’d better keep your nose out of Southern business. Or they’ll take everything you own. Right down to yer under-britches,” he said, then laughed and turned away.

He pointed toward the wagon train and we headed off, back toward the camp with our most recent capture.

At the end of that little raid, I liked to tell other horses that I had seen battle. But the raid was nothing compared to the battles that were yet to come.

Tucker

I heard a shriek that seemed to go through one of my ears and out the other, reverberating through my body as though I could feel the pain that procured the shriek myself. The air smelled of smoke; smoke and blood. Shrapnel exploded through the air and flew toward us like angry bees, and men and horses slammed into each other, trying to avoid becoming a target.

My stiff knees crackled and threatened to buckle from under me from the bitterly cold night before that held little sleep, and the exhaustion that faced me today. Still I tried my best to obey every one of Ben's commands. Several times I had worried about him getting hit, and my nervousness grew with each man I saw fly backwards as a bullet tore through his flesh.

Ben seemed to be alright, and as the day wore on I became even more worried for myself as I saw the horses fall. When I was not completely consumed by worrying where the next bullet would be coming from, I actually admired many of the horses who took the fall for their masters.

I wasn't able to tell who was ahead for a long time. There seemed to be nothing but mass confusion going on as the blue and the gray clashed with each other, constantly attacking one another.

Many times Ben would dismount so that he could get a better shot, trying his best to keep me close by. I fought the urge to run and stayed by his side, forcing myself to focus on Ben and where he was at rather than the confusion going on around me. Dirt, sweat and dried blood covered his face and his curly hair, helping him match the background around him.

By late morning, I could tell that he was becoming even more exhausted. But I could also see that the Rebs were beginning to thin out.

As they began retreating, Ben turned to look at me, wiping his mouth on his dusty sleeve, making a large white spot around his mouth. "Water," he seemed to mouth, and started making his way toward a spot where he might be able to find some.

A man ran past him and grabbed ahold of his blue coat. "Come on, man! Ben, they're retreating! We've got this!"

Ben weakly pushed him away and continued on his search, one hand still on the long split reins. He collapsed under a tree next to another soldier. He panted tiredly, before he looked up. I saw his eyes grow wide as he realized who he was kneeling next to.

A man in a butternut gray uniform held his side, blood leaking through his fingers. His eyes were squinted, as if there was sunlight streaming into his eyes from the cover of the trees above. Each breath was laboriously procured, and it was painful for me to even look at him.

Ben jumped back instinctively when he realized that he was next to a Southern soldier. The man opened his eyes as he heard Ben move, his brown eyes glassy with pain.

"Here to put me out of my misery, Yank?" the soldier asked disgustedly.

Ben shook his head. "Water," he said weakly.

The soldier closed his eyes again and reached for his side, pulling out a metal canteen before he shook it lightly.

Ben hesitated for a moment, then grabbed it quickly out of the man's hands. As he did, his eyes instinctively fell to the man's feet. Where his leg should have been was a gnarled stump that laid in a pool of blood. Ben began to gag quietly, but stopped almost as suddenly as he had started. He retreated back, holding the canteen carefully. "Thank you," he said softly.

"God forgive me for helpin' out a Yank," the other soldier pleaded, before his head rolled to the side and he took his final breath.

Ben stared in shock for a moment, wondering if what he saw just really happened in front of his eyes. He finally seemed to shake himself out of the trance and stood up, gulping the water out of the canteen greedily.

He turned back to look at the advancing line of U.S. soldiers in front of him; the wave of blue that was overtaking the retreating group of gray. The flag carrier rushed ahead of him, holding the Stars and Stripes out in victory.

Ben grabbed the front of the saddle and climbed aboard my back, kicking me into a gallop. He pulled out his rifle from his scabbard and aimed, his fire deadly.

Near noon, I heard the cry "Victory!" Never had I heard such a lovely word in my life. The southern forces that had not retreated had been captured, and the gray began to completely dissolve from the battle field.

Ben and I, along with the other soldiers, pursued them for awhile until we knew that the entire force had been beaten. Many of the Graybacks had been captured, and the rest where nowhere to be seen on the field, retreating east.

Ben and I trotted back towards where the wounded were beginning to be treated by the army's doctors and nurses in a small barn near the field. Even from a distance I could tell that it was a place that I wouldn't want to be in. Shrieks could be heard from inside from those who received amputations or other painful types of treatment.

I could hardly believe such a violent and vulgar thing could exist in such an otherwise peaceful environment. The Arkansas air was still a little cold from the March wind, but the sun shone brightly down on the field and the men that were in it. The long grass stood trampled down in most areas, but in others it stayed alert, waving peacefully in the wind.

"James!" Ben interrupted my thoughts as he tried to get another soldier's attention.

"Do you know where Phillip is?" he asked urgently.

"Mr. Carter?" the man asked.

Ben nodded his head in affirmation. "I need to talk to him."

"Hold on, I'll see if he's busy."

A few minutes later, a man emerged from the barn, dressed in an apron covered in blood. "You needed to see me?"

Ben dropped the reins and went inside, to talk to Philip about whatever it was that he needed to see him for.

I stayed outside of the barn for awhile, anxiously awaiting Ben's return. The atmosphere sickened me. I couldn't stay there for much longer and so I left, the long reins dragging beneath my feet as I patiently began to walk across the field. I would be back before Ben would anyway, and if I wasn't; well, he would find me.

Not many people paid attention to a wandering horse, as there were many others riderless in the field, some of them taking shelter beneath the trees, swishing flies away with their tails. Others were wounded and laid on the ground, either making pitiful noises or calmly awaiting a human to come for them or for what their fate would be.

I sought another horse to offer me comfort and company at this strange time. I didn't see any that I knew and I did not feel obligated to talk to those I didn't.

Soon, however, my attention was drawn to a brown paint horse spinning in a circle, the reins tangling under its feet as is piteously grunted and shook its head. Blood dripped from behind the horse's ears almost down into its eyes, and the horse was limping in the kind of way that you knew never ended well for a horse.

I moved up from my casual walk to a slow trot. There was nothing I could do for the horse and I wanted to get away from the chaos in front of me.

I stopped in shock as I passed and got a better look.

The horse was Catori.

Shiloh

"STICK 'EM UP, BOYS!"

Even though the train was standing still, it still seemed to creak and moan like a living animal. The conductor and engineer stood outside of the engine, their hands in the air.

"Whatda we got here?" Jerry asked, "supplies for yer Yankee brethren?"

We seemed to be on a different raid every day. The live-each-day-as-it-comes life seemed to sit well with Sarah. She loved being able to support the Rebel cause, in her own way; she was winning a little bit more of the war each day. I enjoyed it too, though I would like to be able to wake up in the morning without wondering if it would be my last day on earth.

All was silent as Jerry walked up to one of the boxcars, flipping the latch on the outside of it with a smile. The conductor and the engineer waited with anticipation, and so did our group of cavalry. What kind of goodies would be inside?

Jerry pushed the boxcar open, a smile on his face. It wasn't the first time that we had been able to stop a train and take what was in it. Sarah leaned forward anxiously in the saddle.

The door slid open.

A shot rang out, and Jerry fell backwards onto the ground. Our men's faces fell open in surprise, before they yanked their horses' reins and kicked spurs into their sides.

More shots.

Shouting men.

Clattering of Yankee boots.

A wave of U.S. soldiers dressed in blue emerged from the boxcar, eagerly anticipating "shootin' some Rebs." There must have been hundreds of them.

The men of the cavalry cut their whips into their horses, trying to get away from the storm of Yanks. They did have the advantage of being on horseback, but there were too many U.S. soldiers for all of them to avoid a bullet. Southern men fell backwards out of their saddles left and right.

Sarah dug her heels into my sides and leaned closer to my neck. It was lucky that she and I both were small; small and fast. It was a little bit harder for the soldiers to hit us.

The volunteer cavalry was scattered as the U.S. soldiers pursued them.

Sarah ran down a bluff and into some trees. Faster and faster we seemed to run, until the clatter and the men's voices became distant and then disappeared. When she believed that we were far enough away, she stopped, and exhaled deeply as she held her side, tears running down her face.

"What are we going to do now, Shiloh?" She asked, with the harsh Missouri wind as our only companion.

We couldn't go back to try to find the rest of the cavalry. That would be suicide at this time. For all we knew, the area was crawling with blue-coated soldiers. Many of the men of the cavalry were dead, maybe all of them. Surely not, though.

Sarah debated where to go, talking to herself softly as I leisurely walked across the prairie grass.

"Well, I'd say the best way ta go is east….east? Right? Dat's where the army of the Mississippi was supposed to be? I cain't 'member.

"Meybe I'll go south. The further south we go, the more likely that we'll be finding some southern sympathizers. Ugh. I need to cut my hair, it's gettin' too long. Wait.. South? West? East? I don't know!"

I snorted and tossed my head. I didn't care where we went, as long as there wasn't anybody shooting at us.

She sighed, and trotted me in the opposite direction of the setting sun.

We must have traveled that way for a couple days. I can't remember. But it was quiet. We didn't run into any Bushwhackers, Jayhawkers, Yanks or Bluebacks. The area was mostly cleared out because of the General Order 11 that was issued by Union General Thomas Ewing. The order required all rural families to leave the area because of the violence perpetuated by the Bushwhackers. So the land we traveled through was vastly empty; the only sign of human life being the occasional abandoned home or the burnt skeleton of one. I ate the long prairie grass that grew in patches of Missouri prairie and Sarah ate whatever she could find, the skills she attained as a farmer's daughter put to good use.

We traveled for days until we finally came to a home that didn't seem to be abandoned. Sarah sat on my back from within the trees of a shelter belt, looking on a farmstead that appeared to be inhabited.

"I don't know what to do," she said softly. "But I don't think I have a choice. I can't keep wandering around until I starve or get killed by a Yank. I need some direction, and some food."

She shrugged her shoulders, and decided to try her luck. She trotted me up into the front yard of the house cautiously. A little girl sat up on the deck; a toddler who was half-dressed ran into the house as soon as she saw us. Sarah gulped nervously, and a minute or so later, a woman walked out of the door.

She took one look at the small, scrawny blond "boy" sitting on the gray horse, dusty, tired, and dressed grayish-brown cotton clothes, and her frown turned into a slight smile.

"Hullo there," she said in a friendly manner. "How can I help ya today, feller?"

Sarah squinted against the sun, her body was leaned forward with her hands resting on the saddle horn, the reins held lightly between her fingers. Her heavy western saddle was covered with dirt, the scabbard at my side held her rifle, and her pistol in her holster. Even the blanket underneath the saddle was blood red with the stars and bars poking out from underneath. There was no doubt to where Sarah held her allegiance.

She took off her wide-brimmed hat before she began to talk to the woman. "Hello, ma'am." Sarah said politely. "My name's Sam. Sam Buford. I lost my regiment awhile back when we were attacked by Yanks. I would be most obliged if you would be willing to point me in the general direction of the Army of the Mississippi under Johnston."

The woman was more than willing to help. "Well, dontcha worry about a thang," she said. "Ya poor child, come inside and clean up for a minute, and I'll find you something to eat. I'll send Charlie out to get my husband. We've got two boys in the army, and though we might not know where they are exactly, I'm sure my husband does have some sort of idea."

Sarah smiled, and tied me to a fence post in the front yard. The windows were open and I was able to hear quite a bit of their conversation from my position outside.

The first things they bothered with were letting Sarah wash herself up a bit and getting her some cornbread, a little bit of coffee and some salted pork. Soon enough a tall dark man passed by me and went inside the house as well. He went inside and Sarah stood respectfully as he entered. They talked about where the Army of the Mississippi would possibly be, and how she could get there.

They also offered her a place to sleep, and a place to keep me. "You can stay in the barn, but you'll have to sleep in the same place where Charlie is. I was hopin' that you wouldn't take offense to that, but we haven't really got room in the house. I wish I had more to offer for someone like you that's been serving our country and all, but I'm sure many a Confederate soldier has slept in a worse place than a barn," the man said with a chuckle.

Sarah agreed. She stayed in the house for a while longer before she came outside and untied me. The sun was beginning to set in the west and the breeze began to pick up a little bit. She tiredly walked toward the barn, her stomach heavy with the food that she had eaten.

She opened the door of the barn. Inside stood a young man, with shining dark skin and dirty gray clothes.

"If'n you want me ta take yer horse for ya, I'd be obliged."

Sarah thought about it for a while before she simply nodded her head, and the boy took the reins out of her hands.

He took me to a small stall that was filled with fresh straw, and uncinched the saddle carefully. He pulled off the saddle and blanket and threw them over a ledge. I lowered my head and the boy pulled the bridle over my ears carefully. He grabbed an old brush and began to work the sweat and burrs out of my coat, softly humming to himself as he moved the brush over my tired hide.

He finished in a timely manner and left the stall quietly. Sarah had already made herself a bed in a clean pile of hay on the other side of the barn, and I could hear her moving a bit as she tried to find a comfortable place to lay.

Her guns and holster laid near her in case she would come to need them. She had learned to sleep like this and there was no sense in changing her habits now.

The boy respectfully continued on his other chores before making himself a bed on the other side of the large pile of hay. Sarah lay awake, her hands behind her head.

The boy snuggled down into the hay without a word, until he got a bit curious and opened his mouth to talk.

"If ya don't mind me askin'...why are you fighting for the Confederates?"

Sarah started when she heard his voice at first, but then leaned up on her side a little bit. "Well, it's complicated. But to make a long story short, we'd be fighting the second revolution. It's says in our Declaration of Independence that 'whenever any form of government becomes destructive of these ends, it is the right of the people to alter or abolish it, and to institute a new government.' And so dat's why we're fighting. The people in Washington are getting too big for their britches and trying to control us. They're the ones tryin' ta make *us* into slaves. We need to create a government that 'llows us to do what's right, Charlie."

Charlie looked thoughtful for a moment before he answered. "But it also says that 'all men are created equal.' How could you fight for a nation that is founded on slavery?"

Sarah shook her head. "That's not the point. It's says nothin' 'bout women in the Declaration either, but you don't see dem all up in a huff, ready ta go ta war over it. Slavery ain't even the point of this war. It's a war to make our men free, not yours."

"Well, how come there are no slaves up north? And how come down south, men are 'llowed to stay at home and not go to war if'n they have more than fifty slaves? I know Missoura isn't really a slave state, with only a few here and there, but I've heard talk of plantations with hundreds of slaves. I couldn't even believe that there would be such a place, but the cruelty and abuse that they say goes on down there is even harder to believe."

Sarah was beginning to lose her temper. "That doesn't even matter. From what I've heard there are slaves in the deep south that eat like kings compared to the poor factory workers in the north.

"I've lived in the south my whole life," Sarah continued. "And yer only the second or third slave I've ever seen. Our men—my brothers and father—they are not out there dying for slavery. They're not."

"Well that's what ya think," he answered, "and I'm not liable to change yer mind. But one day you Rebs will git it through your head that a nation cannot exist half slave and half free."

Sarah huffed, and turned in the straw to face away from him, feeling like she was losing the argument. "You don't understand is all," she said softly. "You and I are just not the same."

Tucker

Late March of 1862

I rushed toward Catori. I couldn't believe that she had been hurt, and I needed to help her in whatever way I could.

She turned when she saw me, her eyes rolled white in fear and shock. "Catori!" I called to her. "What happened?"

She snorted. "I don't know, I don't know…Michael and I were hit by fragments of the artillery…I need to get out of here."

"Calm down," I tried to reassure her, though my mind was racing. If her leg was broken she wouldn't have much to look forward to.

"Let me look at your foreleg," I told her calmly. I leaned down to take a look, and my heart felt relief like I had never felt before.

Fragments of shrapnel had implanted itself in her foreleg, up through her shoulder and neck; and she had managed to step on a harsh piece of metal, one end stuck through her heel. But her leg was straight, no sign of anything broken.

I had to get her to someone who knew how to care for horses. I knew Ben was good with equine care, but would he be able to take care of Catori?

"Catori, do you think that you'd be able to walk?"

She looked up and shook her head. "I won't be able to go far."

I snorted. "You can do it Catori. You're a strong horse."

"I can't!" she replied helplessly. "Those Rebs got me and now I'm going to die out here on this field."

I was quiet for a moment as I looked at her worriedly. Flies buzzed around us in the field and made their way from bodies to live horses and men, seemingly bothering everyone but Catori. The sun was hanging low in the sky by now, and I knew that if I didn't bring her to camp the nighttime predators would be out to bother her until she gave up.

I took a deep breath and walked up to her, putting my head on her withers. "You've got to pull through, Catori. I know you can do it. And if you can't do it for you, do it for me."

She looked surprised but somehow it seemed to knock some sense into her. She took a deep breath and then moved forward, limping along in an odd kind of way, but moving fast enough to surprise me.

It took us a long time, nonetheless. I was trying to lead her back to where I thought Ben was, but it was a lot harder than I expected, with people running and walking back and forth, loose horses kicking up dust, still imagining the terror in their minds, and carts coming along to begin cleaning up the mess on the battlefield.

We came to the barn as the sun was setting. "Stay here, Catori," I told her. "I'm going to try to find Ben."

I trotted away and frantically looked for Ben, while hoping not to be caught by a curious soldier.

I was finally able to see his curly mop of hair above some of the others and I trotted toward him. He was talking to someone at the time, and so I put my nose on the back of his shoulder.

He turned around with a gentle swat ready, but when he saw it was me, he stopped. "Tucker? What's up boy?"

I pushed my nose into him, trying to get him to come with me.

He pushed my nose back. "Not right now, boy," he said. "I'm busy."

He turned around and continued to talk to the other man, but I was intent on getting his attention. I moved in front of him, and pushed my nose into him until he pushed me back again. "Get away!" He shooed me away.

But I considered this matter urgent, and he had already had half of the day to attend to his needs. I finally stepped around him, and right onto his foot.

"OWWwww! What do you want, horse?"

I finally had his attention and tried to get him to follow me. He finally gave up and sighed, exasperated. "Excuse me," he told the other man, and grabbed the reins, threw a foot into the stirrup, and climbed on my back. He kicked my sides, frustrated, and I jumped into a lope. He was surprised, but held on to the saddle and urged me forward.

I brought him to the place where Catori was, and he gasped softly when he saw her. He climbed off my back, went over to her, and put a hand on her shoulder to steady her.

"Shhh," he softly whispered. "It'll be okay."

He picked up her leg and bent it at the joints, testing for a break before he did anything.

He looked back at me, in awe that I had brought him over to where Catori was, but didn't seem to question it. "She'll be okay, boy," he said to me. "If I doctor her up, I think she'll pull through." And with that, he grabbed my reins and led her back to where the other horses were picketed. He took hold of my reins as well but I would have followed them no matter where they were going.

By now it was dusk and Ben had to work quickly if he wanted to finish with any amount of light to see by. He unsaddled Catori and me, and then washed her wounds with utmost care, but also watching out for himself as Catori jumped and fidgeted. He bandaged them with a few strips of the cleanest cloth that he could find. When he was finished, he picketed the two of us a short distance away from the rest of the horses. Catori closed her eyes, drifting into a deep kind of sleep from the exhausting day that we had just experienced.

I found my eyes closing a few times, but I shook the exhaustion from my head every time that I heard the coyotes and wolves howling in the distance. They knew what was going on and would be ready to clean up whatever was left over, a wounded horse wouldn't be hard for them to make a meal out of either. I wanted to stay up and watch Catori. I didn't know why I felt like I had to watch over her, but I did. I just wanted her to be alright.

The next morning, Ben came out with another man to check up on Catori and me. I snorted as they approached us.

The other man was a General.

"He's been next to her all night," Ben explained to him. "It's almost like he cares for her and wants to help her get better." He smiled a little.

The general, however, was looking mostly at me. I could tell that he admired my tall, muscular frame and my dark bay color. He put a hand on my shoulder and smoothed it down carefully.

"He is a very fine horse, indeed," he said to Ben. "I managed to see you and this horse in battle yesterday. Many of the horses were frightened and ran away, or were too brave and shot down. This horse seems to have common sense."

"Why, of course," Ben acknowledged. "He's the best mount I've had in the Federal army. Well, he's the best horse I've ever had."

"I can see that," the officer answered. "And he's beautiful. With a little more training, he will be everything that a person wants in a war horse."

Ben looked a little confused, but didn't say anything else to the General.

The general continued. “And that is why I am re-assigning the fellow. Tucker, did you say his name was?”

The smile was disappearing from Ben’s face little by little. “Yes, sir. That’s his name.”

“Very good. Colonel Grayson will definitely be able to appreciate this horse.”

I stayed with Catori for as long as I was allowed to. The night after Ben had doctored her wounds, I stood with her near the pickets, somehow seeming to be able to tell that this was the last day that I would be able to see her as much as I had been.

“Catori?” I said softly in the calm night air.

“Yes,” she answered quietly, though she seemed a little startled.

“Do you think you’re going to be okay?” I asked.

“I will be,” she said, “thanks to you.”

I sighed. “Do you think that I will be able to see you very often as soon as I am ‘reassigned’?” I asked.

“I don’t know. But I don’t want to think about you leaving me. You’ve been one of the best friends I’ve had since this war started.”

I sighed. “I really hope that I’ll still be able to see you. I thought you were a bit of a know-it-all when I first met you. But now I understand more about how you really are.”

She smiled and nuzzled the side of my check. I turned away, embarrassed, but hiding a smile of my own.

“I don’t know if I’ll be able to see you very much, but I’ll try to whenever I can.”

I saw Ben coming up from behind the trees to take one of the horses out and I had a good feeling that it was me. He un-looped the halter from the picket line and pulled my head away.

I followed him quietly without worrying about where we were going. It was up to fate now, and only time would tell what could happen next in my story.

I was a true war-horse now. Or at least closer to being a true war horse than the days before the Battle of Pea Ridge. I had seen the Elephant, and I had proved myself courageous in battle. Or at least that I could pretend to be courageous enough to fool the humans.

More men joined our army everyday as we prepared to meet a large force of Confederates sometime in the future. That was all I knew about any upcoming battles.

There seemed to be men and horses everywhere. I could never imagine all these people gathered at one time for any other reason—the war changed a lot of things. There were men here from Ohio, Iowa, Nebraska, Missouri, Minnesota, Kentucky, Illinois, and other states. Men who had grown up in the area as well as immigrants. Some of them were farmers, some were doctors, still others were shop clerks or railroad men. It's hard to believe that they could all get along with all of their different backgrounds, but they had all united for the common cause—their fight for freedom and their fight to keep the nation together. And so they stuck together, and somehow the generals and other commanders of the army kept them under control and going in the right direction.

A lot of men had heard about how good I was in battle, even though I was considered "inexperienced" in battle as far as horses went. I had stayed close to Ben's side no matter what was happening throughout my first encounter with battle. A lot of the men came to look at the great war horse, give me a pat and maybe a treat if I was lucky. There were all different kinds of men—men with southern accents, with northern ones, foreign ones, men with dark hair, dark skin, blond hair, light skin, tall and short, young boys and old men.

But none of them quite amounted to the new master that I would have—Lieutenant Colonel William Grayson. He was a lot different from Ben. He was born in Kentucky but raised in Illinois, and was a veteran of past Indian wars. He was tough as nails and one would only have to look at him to know it.

When he was younger he had lost his arm in a farming accident and had to have it amputated. Even so, it didn't stop him from leaving his job as a sheriff and entering the Union Army.

Unless a horse was an exceptional equine, it would usually switch hands many times throughout the course of the battles of this Civil War. But, the Lieutenant took a liking to me and hoped to keep me for awhile. I didn't mind this arrangement, though I didn't get to see Catori as much as I would have liked to, Ben would still help care for me as well as the other horses, and would allow me to be tethered next to Catori sometimes.

Another advantage to being a Lieutenant's horse was that I heard and understood more about the upcoming battles and war strategies. Though it still was confusing to me, it was made a little clearer as I was exposed more to it.

"The Graybacks are believed to be gathering at Corinth," I heard a General speaking to the Lieutenant.

"Indeed. They may be rebellious but not completely unintelligent. They realize that the town is a major artery in the heartland of the South, with the railroad junction there." The Lieutenant scratched his long, graying beard as he spoke, deep in thought. "I believe that originally Halleck planned on tearing up some railroad line down there. But he's changing his mind to produce a full-scale attack."

"They're waiting for us at Savannah," the General reminded my master. "We need to get down there to support Grant."

So, if the mind between my two little horse-ears was working right, the North was on the offensive. They planned to strike the heart of the South in Corinth, Mississippi while tearing up railroad line along the way so that the Rebs couldn't as well supply their vast armies.

Seemed easy enough.

The marching was not.

We marched for days, again, until we came to Savannah, where we learned that the encampment would be on Pittsburg Landing.

The place seemed ideal for an offensive encampment—the landing was protected from both the north and southeast by the Owl and Snake Creek to the north, and the Lick Creek to the southwest. Swampy and moccasin snake-infested, they would provide a fairly impenetrable barrier against the Confederates. Along with the rushing Tennessee River to our backs, we could be assured that we would be protected from Confederate attack. Or so we thought.

Shiloh

Sarah was off as soon as the sun had started to rise. Her breath and mine came out in little puffs of steam, as the early spring morning had awhile yet to warm up. Yellow fingers of sunlight stretched through the budding trees, over the barn and farmhouse where we were staying. The family was still asleep yet and so was Charlie.

Sarah saddled me in silence, her face thoughtful, but twisted into a slight frown as she tightened the cinch. Her hair was still growing a little long, I thought that she should probably cut it before she became in danger of looking just a little bit too feminine and people would begin asking questions. Sarah's face was a bit dirty still even though she had washed it the evening before, her white-blond hair falling into her eyes.

She had always been tough and strong, "for a girl," as the saying went. But now she looked even more so. Her trim figure started to fill out with muscles as she spent most of her time riding, fighting or drilling.

But she had yet to see actual battle.

The thought worried me a little as she finished saddling up and climbed aboard, kicking me into a lope.

Sarah talked to me—or rather, more to herself—as we loped along.

"The man there, Daniel, I think his name was, said that the Confederate forces are concentratin' in Corinth. It's quite a ways away from here, yet, but we should be able to make it there in time to see some action. Think about it, Shiloh. The chance ta be able to actually *fight* under the flag. With thousands of other men in their gray cotton uniforms. It'll really be somethin'."

It would be something. Something that, at the time, we wouldn't be able to even begin to imagine.

We traveled along alone for a few days without running into any trouble, which was surprising in this kind of territory.

After a while we did run into a group of traveling Rebs. Not a large group, maybe twenty or thirty men and about forty horses and mules, but enough to know where they were going and what for.

"To the west and the south!" they cheered, "on to Corinth!" I found it interesting how no matter where Sarah went, wherever there were Rebs, all she had to do is show her support for the gray and she was accepted nearly at once.

There was a strong sense of family coursing through the veins of the Rebels. They were brothers, all fighting for their homeland, for their women, their freedom and for their cause.

We trotted along in good spirits, and I couldn't remember if the group of men bothered to call themselves a regiment or not, but they tried to act like it a little. None of the men had seen battle before, maybe a skirmish or two if they were lucky, but nothing big enough to be considered "real."

As it turned out, this kind of men would be the type that would make up the larger Army of the Mississippi, under Beauregard and Johnston. Men who had never "seen the Elephant," as the saying goes, greener than a new blade of grass in the early spring dew.

As we traveled, some of the men talked with Sarah, impressed with what she knew so far about the fighting. They would have been more impressed had they known she was a girl.

We plodded along, the late March air warming and encouraging us on our journey. "I can't wait til we git to Corinth," Sarah was saying to one of the men as she rode alongside him. “It seems like I’ve spent all dis time in littl’ spats that haven’t helped our cause one bit. Well, take that back. They did help a little, I do believe, but not much. I’m ready to see real battle.”

The man beside her nodded. “It would be good if’n we were able to fight those yellerbellies, either a few or more at a time.”

“Tell me more ‘bout what you know about the Army of the Mississippi,” Sarah interrupted.

“Well,” he started, scratching his moustache, “It is led of course by Beauregard and Johnston. I ain’t sure of their particular achievements in the battlefields, but they are good generals nonetheless. Though Johnston is in command, and Beauregard is second, they team up more likely to be co-commanders—it’s the Southern way of doing things, really. I’ve heard that Beauregard is in bad health. Fevers and infections and such. Doctors told him that he should be on bedrest but he continues to ride and fight beside his men—and that’s the Southern way too. He’s a Frenchman. They say he rides in a fancy uniform with a spiffy red cap. Oh well. He fights like a Southern man any way around it. Johnston’s a little more sensible.”

Flies began to buzz around us. I couldn’t believe that they were out already, it should have been too cold for them yet, but they bothered the horses nonetheless and we shook our manes and occasionally scratched our heads on our forelegs if our riders would let us get away with it. But the man that rode beside Sarah continued on.

“I guess that the army had been divided into four corps. I’m not sure what corps we will belong to, but we’ll find out soon as we git there. Lemme see here—there’s Bragg, I heard he’s a sultry man. Hopefully, we don’t get stuck with him as our officer. Hardee of course, ‘Old Reliable’ they call him. Polk—I believe that they call him “The Fighting Bishop,” since he originally was a bishop of some fancy church, and then there's Breckinridge. I'm not sure of very much about him except for the fact that he fought in the Mexican War. But that's not so much of a big deal in these parts, since many of our officers are veterans of that war."

Sarah nodded while rearranging her split reins above the saddle horn, taking it all in. "So what are Johnston and Beauregard plannin' to do to git the Yanks?"

The man looked at her, and then leaned forward. "Well, I don't think anyone is a hundred percent sure at this time," he said. "Most people believe that the Yanks are settled down under Grant at Pittsburg Landing. That would leave them only about twenty miles away from where our men are. The plan would be to march the twenty miles to the landing and attack them—by surprise, of course, if possible. And chase their yeller men into their demise in the swampy Owl and Snake Creek bottoms."

Sarah nodded again. It sounded like a good plan to her. At least it *sounded* like one.

"Sometimes I wonder if these battles even matter that much," she said out loud. "It seems that the news from east is so much bigger than it is out here. Open fire, battle, and acts of defiance on Fort Sumter. Thousands dead or wounded in the Battle of Manassas. Big politicians with their big talk. It seems like sometimes all we have out here are ruffians lookin' for a fight."

The man shook his head. "There is a lot at stake here. I believe that these western fights will be more important than anyone can imagine."

In a few weeks' travel, we had reached the army's encampment in Corinth, Mississippi. There were tents set up everywhere, men and horses crowded in the area. I could hardly keep calm with all of the bustling that was going on in the area. I had never seen so many people or horses in one place, with men present from nearly the entire Confederacy. This was the first time that Sarah and I had ever even seen an actual army of this size, and we gaped upon entering the encampment.

The place buzzed with excitement, the men chomping at their bits to see real battle. It would be amazing—it would be wonderful—it would be the chance for the boys and men to either prove themselves as war heroes or forever be shamed as cowards. Oh, good gravy. Apparently there was nothing as shameful to these Rebs than to be called a coward.Their honor, their families, their very *manliness* itself would depend on how they faced the battle.

"I'll shoot up every single one of those Yankees 'til the shots can be heard clear up in Washington!"

"I'll throw 'em in a washtub and scrape every last bit of Yank out of 'em and every bit o yeller out of their belly until they'd be as clean as a Reb—then I'd shoot 'em."

The talk went on like that everywhere in the camp. In fact, I got sick of hearing about how every one of them was going to string up a Yank and butter up their toast with Yank insides.

If war could be won by talk, I'm sure that it would have been over by now and the Confederate States of America would be alive and thriving on all that talk.

Our little regiment was assigned to Hardee, and Sarah and I were glad. "Old Reliable" was a respected yet fair and kind general, veteran of the Mexican War, and an author of a drill manual called *Hardee's Tactics* that was said to be used by both the Northern and Southern generals.

Special Order Number Eight—I heard a lot about that in the first few days that we were in Corinth. Johnston, Beauregard, and Colonel Thomas Jorden were the ones who had written up the order, which outlined the battles, the details of which weren't exactly clear to the soldiers, much less the horses, but I heard it had something to do with Napoleon's battle plan at Waterloo. It sounded quite bookish to me and I wondered if it would actually work when applied to real life.

The beginning part of the order required us to march to Pittsburg Landing to the Yanks' encampment, where we would surprise them, fight a little, and win easily.

The order would end up being quite the failure, but at the time we weren't aware of it. The first part of our order was the march. Johnston and Beauregard allowed for one day to march from Corinth to the landing. A mere twenty miles.

There were only two roads leading to the area where the Yankees were—the Ridge Road and The Montery Road. The order of march put Polk and Hardee on one road, and Bragg and Breckinridge on the other.

It was easier said than done. I didn't know it at the time, and neither did Sarah or many of the other men, but the amount of soldiers, officers, teamsters, doctors, and other men that traveled in the Army of the Mississippi was made of more than forty-thousand people. Forty thousand people!

It was harder than the generals had imagined to move all those people, not to mention the thousands of horses and mules that accompanied the men.

At this point in the war, no one really understood how to move that many people effectively. The troops were raw and weren't used to marching.

And not only that, only a few hours into the march, the skies opened and started to rain like I've never seen before. It started out by coming down in sheets, soaking and chilling the men and horses.

You might wonder, what's wrong with a little rain? Well, even a little rain would have been a problem with all of these men and animals, wagons and other traffic. But this was incredible. With all of the traffic, the roads became a gooey, slippery, filthy mess. Wagons and artillery got stuck and caused hour-long delays, men and horses fell into the sticky mud, clothes and shoes got filthy and filled with mud. The early April rain continued on for days, and it hailed on and off, pelting the men and the horses.

I plodded on through the weather with Sarah on my back at times, and with her on the ground at other times, as she tried to convince me to cross a particularly water-covered path in such a way to avoid getting stuck. My fur soaked all the way through in the first few hours of our journey, and the other horses and I seemed to eternally be a shade darker than usual. We stayed that way for days.

There was mud on my forelegs and hind legs all the way up to my hocks and knees. I almost looked a little bit more like my brother, I thought, when I looked down at the bottom half of my legs. I hadn't thought about Tucker for a long time. I wondered what he was doing, and if he was alive.

Of course he was alive. He was my brother, after all. Like me but bigger, stronger, and probably smarter. I entertained ideas of what happened to him, but I couldn't be sure. To set my mind at ease I had decided that he had found an excellent home—that the man who had bought him brought him home to a wife and children in a cabin somewhere, away from this fighting. His master would have gotten out of the fighting somehow, and if his master did have to fight in the war, he wouldn't have brought Tucker with him.

I missed the days when we used to play together. Thinking back I thought we seemed decades younger, even though it had really only been a few months since I had seen him. I remembered galloping around the pastureland, play biting and kicking each other, not worrying about anything except for hurt feelings. My whole family was there, and it seemed a million times more peaceful than what was going on in my life now.

Looking back, I could still see Tucker's tall dark form, my friend, my brother, my protector. My mother trotting out from the shed to meet us after a fight. I let my mind wander.

I was brought back into reality when a splash of freezing water blasted into my face and into my eyes, dripping down my long nose into my nostrils. A young buckskin filly had been spooked by something and jumped ahead and into the other horses, splashing water everywhere.

"You there!" One of the men yelled to the man on the filly. "Keep your hoss under control!"

The rain began to get even more annoying and depressing at the same time. Oh, when would it stop?

Men waited for hours for crossings to clear, for things to get unstuck, for the soldiers in front of them to move. It was terrible. Johnston had originally planned on the attack to occur on the fourth of April, but because of delays he pushed it to the fifth. And then the sixth. We seemed to be managing little more than five miles a day, when a horse and rider on a good day would make twenty miles or more.

If that wasn't bad enough, the men ran out of rations on the fifth. They had been issued what the generals considered five days' rations at the beginning of the march but since they were not used to rationing food, the green soldiers ate their supply of flour and grease biscuits before they reached the landing. Sarah and the other soldiers would be fighting on empty stomachs.

Sarah sat in a wrapped blanket waiting for a portion of the army to move. It had seemed to be in the same place for the last hour or more. She held one of the reins in her hand and held the blanket in place around her with the other hand, her short wet hair plastered to her head, and shaking with cold.

A shot rang off and I jumped, but Sarah held the rein tightly and calmed me down quickly.

“Stupid boys,” a man who sat next to her shook his head angrily.

“What are they doing?” Sarah asked cautiously.

“Well, some of them aren’t certain if their powder still works after being soaked with all this rain.” He huffed. “Well, they know it works now. But the Yanks probably do now, too. I know Johnston wanted a surprise attack, but he’s never going to get it now with all this blasted noise. Those Yanks would have to be dead already if they haven’t heard all the noise from our boys!”

Sarah put her head down on her knees, tired of being cold and hungry.

“Cheer up, boy,” the man told her gently. “We should be ready to attack the Yanks tomorrow. And there’s rumors about that there’s a chance that we might actually be marching back to Corinth, considering how badly this march has been going, anyway.”

“I don’t care either way,” Sarah said, “as long as this cursed rain stops sometime soon.”

Late on the evening of the fifth, Beauregard, backed up by most of the corps commanders, urged Johnston to call the entire thing off. Based on how badly the march alone was going, it might not have been a bad idea.

What was Johnston to do? Was he to send his army forward against the advice of his co-commander and most of his generals? Send his men into a possible trap and disaster? The results would be his responsibility.

He wasn’t sure what to do at first, and pondered the decision for awhile, until he stiffened and said, “I would fight them if they were a million.”

Tucker

April 6, 1862 (Approximately 3am-6am)

A group of riders rode into our camp, furiously loping toward Colonel Peabody's campsite. The lieutenant saw the commotion and grabbed my reins from where I was tied with his good arm, and mounted, kicking me to follow the other horses.

He stopped when he saw them talking to the Colonel.

"I'm telling you. We spotted them. Graybacks. We saw a squad of Rebel cavalry. And what were they doing? Just sitting on their horses. *Watching us.*"

Peabody scratched his beard. "Why would they be allowed so close to a Federal encampment? Aren't they wary of us, or are they not bothered by it?"

"I'm not sure," the man answered him.

"But you know that Grant is getting sick and tired of hearing about enemy sightings. He says he has no worries about it, and threatened to have the next person who says anything about any Graybacks shot."

"But why would they be so close?"

"I'm not sure," Peabody answered, "I suppose we'll just have to wait and find out."

But it turned out that even Peabody wouldn't want to wait to find out. The next afternoon, a few men of the 25th Missouri under Peabody noticed a group of enemy cavalry, again simply observing us.

Later that same day, the 25th Missouri again had doubt sown into their minds. While patrolling along a road toward Seay Field, a now-abandoned cotton field, they encountered a few slaves, who claimed that early in the day they had seen a large group of Confederate soldiers.

But, the soldiers themselves hadn't truly seen anything and so there was nothing they could really do about it, though many of the 25th Missouri swore that they heard thrashing in the woods.

The Rebels were like ghosts, traveling right through the forest and fields around us, their threatening presence seemingly always there but never truly visible. When would we actually come in contact with the Confederate army?

It was dark and chilly that night, with only a quarter moon that was occasionally covered by clouds to darken it. Crickets and other bugs made noises from within their realms of the dark fields and forests. The camp was quiet, even though it was full of thousands of soldiers. Even so, I couldn't sleep. I was worrying about the Rebel soldiers. How they seemed to be everywhere and nowhere all at once. I just couldn't seem to be able to forget about them. Fog rose up over the large Tennessee River, floating into the camp and creating a generally spooky feeling.

I felt a hand on my shoulder. A few horses picketed beside me jumped, but I wasn't spooked. I was able to see the outline of a curly mop of hair and so I knew it was Ben. He threw a heavy cavalry saddle on my back, and I wondered why he had decided to take me and where we were going.

I would soon find out. It had turned out that Peabody couldn't forget about the Rebel sightings, either. He just couldn't. He laid awake until he finally decided that it was time to once and for all figure out if there truly was a Rebel army out there.

He had ordered another general—Major Powell—to form one last patrol to help set his mind at ease. Powell had gathered about

200 soldiers to go with him on the patrol. An unauthorized patrol. Many grumbled and complained about being awakened in the middle of the night, but most of the men were from Powell's own 25th Missouri, and so there was nothing they could do but follow orders.

The sleepy men mounted their horses and marched down the same road that the Rebels had been patrolling on the previous day, toward Seay Field again.

It was so dark that one could hardly see the riders in front of him. The men were drowsy, but tried to stay alert.

The horses were the only creatures that seemed to make any noise as we walked down the road, their feet thudding, spurs and bits jangling, and snorts and sneezes from a few of them.

The men were quiet as well, except for the occasional whisper shared between a couple of them. Many of them had one hand on the reins with the other on their guns, ready to draw. The Rebels could be anywhere.

A branch snapped loudly.

One of the Federals beside us quickly turned his horse and we heard a shot ring out.

More shots.

The horses and the men jumped. There was a minor commotion among the men and the horses scattered around. A few of the men yelled into the darkness.

Ben reached for his pistol, but didn't take it out, breathing slowly as he tried to tell from which direction the shooting would be coming from.

But when the men realized that there were no Rebels in the direct area and that the shots were only coming from each other, the commotion stopped.

Powell quickly rode up toward men.

"What in the tarnation is going on here?!" He yelled, his voice reverberating through the forest. "We're already spooked enough. You keep this up and the Rebs won't even have to kill ya, you'll do it yourselves."

The men looked down, ashamed, while others simply looked away, and some had yet to put away their guns.

I could hardly see his face in the half-light of the moon, but I guessed that Powell's face was probably turning beet-red by now. "Besides," he continued, "how would I explain to Grant that I had my own regiment shoot themselves up on a patrol that I wasn't even authorized to proceed with?"

He harrumphed, and trotted away on his tall black horse. The men were embarrassed, but started to feel a little more at ease after they had discovered that, as of yet, there was nothing to worry about.

They continued down the road until they reached the Seay Field. The field was nearly black, with scrubby cotton plants rising up from the soil. Since it had no food value it remained untouched by either Federal or Rebel troops, but that was about to change as we marched over it. Without many trees it was easier to see through the darkness.

"There!" Ben whispered to the man that was beside him. "Do you see anything over there at all?"

The man's gaze followed where Ben was pointing, and I looked over too. A few hundred feet away we saw the shadows of three soldiers on horseback.

We saw them before they saw us, but only by a few seconds. Surprised, the riders fired three quick shots..

Bang, bang, BANG!—and galloped away.

The men were now wide awake as Powell rode through the men on horseback, forming them into a long skirmish line.

"We got 'em boys," he encouraged them. "We have confirmed that they are out here, now let's confirm how many of 'em they've got!"

We formed a long line of soldiers and began to march forward, any cotton plants or brush being smashed beneath our powerful hooves.

We could only march for so long until we collided with something that was as strong as we were. A few hundred yards in, we found enemy outposts. They saw us soon enough, and fired a few rounds before galloping away.

I wondered where they were going, until I saw a line of dozens of soldiers coming our way.

A rush of adrenaline flew through my body and my stomach seemed to sink. I fought the urge to run away like mad, quietly advancing forward under Ben's steady hand.

Both sides began firing in earnest as they began to grasp exactly what was going on.

As we marched forward and began firing, somehow I became less anxious and more excited. My hooves began to prance back and forth, working with Ben to keep us both safe from flying bullets.

The bullets sounded like angry wasps at first, buzzing around my head and whizzing past my ears without me being able to actually catch sight of them.

Compared to what I had seen at Pea Ridge, this was nothing. A few hundred men randomly firing off shots in the dark, hoping to hit something? Piece of cake, so far.

We skirmished for about an hour, dodging bullets and returning fire, a few of our men being hit but none dangerously wounded.

As the morning sun began to peak up from behind the hills, the men noticed that the Rebel cavalry was about to try to curl around our left flank. Throughout the little skirmish Powell had been riding through the blue-coated soldiers, encouraging them and urging them on.

But now, I heard the piercing call of the bugle. It was calling the retreat. I wondered why for a few minutes. Or seconds. I can't remember. But I do remember looking up to the hill on the other side of the field, where thousands of gray-coated soldiers could be seen marching directly toward us.

We rushed away from the approaching line of rebels, galloping back toward our camp. My long legs overcame those of the other horses, my unwounded rider urging me forward with every stride.

I was still not afraid, but I understood the bugle calls by now. I knew when it was not wise to stay on the battlefield.

We blasted into our camp, loping through the Sibley tents while trying to avoid men and animals. Powell had sent us orders to deliver the message to Prentiss and Peabody.

We cantered right into a raging fight between the two of them. "Still, what do you think that you could possibly achieve by sending a patrol?" We saw Brigade General Prentiss spitting at Peabody, infuriated that he would take such measures without permission. "I'll tell you what you've achieved. Nothing but riling up those darn Rebs and starting a battle we may not be ready for!"

"Sir!" Ben interrupted the fighting men, "I have been ordered by Major Powell to inform you that his force is being driven back by an enemy force of approximately 3,000 Confederate soldiers."

Both of the men stopped talking and gazed at us in amazement. Prentiss nodded. "You may return to your post, then. We need to decide how we will go about this."

Ben yanked my head around and we trotted back to his area of the camp and to the pickets where he had gotten me from. The Lieutenant was there waiting for us.

“What do you think you’re doing, young man, stealing my horse?” he asked in all seriousness, and I felt Ben go stiff in nervousness.

“Sir,” he said quietly. “I’m sorry. Peabody commanded us out for a patrol, and I didn’t trust my mount in the darkness and under fire. I supposed that it would be fine for me to take Tucker out since he’s as steady as they come.”

The lieutenant snorted. “Without my permission?”

“I had supposed that we would be back before daylight.”

“It doesn’t matter,” the lieutenant snapped. “This horse is still under my charge. And the least you could do is ask for permission, though it is doubtful that I would ever give it to you now.” The lieutenant’s dark face unsettled even me. He could be a very intimidating man at times. Well, most of the time he was intimidating.

“No matter,” he continued. “We need to figure out what exactly is going on. Our biggest concern now is whether your patrol has just fought a skirmish that is over, or if there is more to come.” By now, shots could still be heard in the distances, resounding through the woods, a faint foreshadowing of what was to come.

“Oh, there is definitely more—” Ben started to say.

“Tie my horse back up and water him, then get back to your camp. The men need to be organized and you do no good where you’re at now.”

Ben agreed and began to unsaddle me. “Leave the saddle on ‘im,” the lieutenant said, his scowling dark eyes never leaving Ben’s form.

Ben did as he was told and then left. After a few moments, the lieutenant climbed onto my back and brought me back to the camp. By this time it was around 7:30, and on a usual day the men would be up and drilling already.

Today, most of the men in this division were gone, and the remainder of the men that had not been involved in the early morning skirmish stood at parade rest in front of the camp, their rifles at their sides. The lieutenant was one of the few men mounted on a horse, the vast majority of the men on foot.

They stood a little dozily, weary from lack of sleep and still not completely sure if they were going to be fighting an army or a few random Confederate soldiers that were scattered around the area.

The sun had already begun to rise, the warm rays of sunlight stretching out over the ground, ready to warm the day. It was that time of year in Tennessee where the days were warm, hot even, while the nights were still cool or cold. I could not wait for the sun to get higher in the sky, so that we could see clearly the faces of our enemy. I didn't like battles at all, but I especially didn't like shots in the dark.

Something strange seemed to awaken the men from their tired stance.

Suddenly, dozens of terrified rabbits scampered into the troops' formation. It wasn't rare to see a cottontail or two hopping along a trail in these woods, but now there were dozens of them—maybe hundreds of them, fleeing from something.

The men stood taller, their rifles shuffling as they stared into the horizon.

Presently, we saw something even stranger. A line of soldiers, thousands of gray-coated soldiers, were marching toward us, blood-red banners flapping in the wind and bayonets glistening.

For a few moments—I truly don't know how long it was, because it seemed like forever—we stood and gaped. We were dumbfounded at the sheer amount of soldiers that were marching directly toward us. It seemed as if nobody believed that there were more than a few hundred of these Rebel soldiers after us, and now we were faced with thousands of them at a time.

They advanced slowly and steadily, and all at once, until the Federals seemed to come alive and time started again, the men raising their guns to their shoulders.

As soon as the Rebels got in range—about 125 yards—the Federal soldiers fired. But the Rebels meant business. Once they were in range, they halted and unleashed a torrent of bullets onto us.

You'd think that our men would be a little braver, but I guess the sheer number of Rebels scared them into running back through the camp like a flock of frightened birds. The lieutenant yelled at the men, trying to convince them to stand their ground before he realized that it was useless.

At first, bullets whizzed around us again. I was becoming used to these storms of bullets, but still they scared me every time. The lieutenant attempted to swing me around the side of the camp and toward the outskirts, away from the fleeing Union soldiers. He wanted to try to help herd the soldiers to another division.

We threaded our way through the teepee-like Sibley tents, through the wall tents of the few officers in the camp, and around the fleeing men.

The firing died down considerably, however, as the Confederate soldiers' battle line became broken as men stopped to plunder things from the tents.

The lieutenant used this to his advantage and pushed his men farther and faster as the Confederate battle line was broken. Peabody galloped around on his horse, frantically shouting. I think I heard him yell once or twice, "Remember Lexington!" He was getting infuriated as he saw his brigade falling apart.

He had been wounded, but still sat atop his horse, yelling at his men. One had to be impressed by his nerve, but his temper did nothing to keep his men in line.

By now, many of the soldiers were fleeing the area to head to the larger Federal encampment or Pittsburg Landing. The lieutenant followed their lead and dug his spurs into my side, urging me faster and faster away from the Confederate battle line.

Shiloh

April 6, 1862 (Approximately 7:30 to 2pm)

The land was soft with spring. The warm sun seemed to massage the men and horses after all the days of cold rain. Flowers were starting to bloom in the beautiful April air and trees were covered in large buds and leaves.

On their leisure time, men swam in the ponds or creeks, sunbathed, played cards or simply laid in the shade, providing a picture of laziness that was soon to come to an end.

Most of the men, being from different areas in the South, were used to the weather, many used to even warmer weather. They scoffed at the men who came from the North. It was said that some from areas like Minnesota or Wisconsin claimed that there could still be snow on the ground in early April.

I could hardly imagine it to be true myself, but that wasn't my main concern. Our main concern was either killing these blue-tailed men or chasing them back to their land of snow.

Our men were lining up for battle, and a charge of excitement seemed to go through them and the horses as we prepared our attack on the Northern soldiers.

Beauregard and Johnston were prepared to launch an attack on the Union soldiers, whether it would be a surprise or not, and whether there were a hundred or a million of them.

I could hardly wait for all the men to organize, but the generals wanted us to be as prepared as possible when the time came for us to actually fight.

As I stood there with the rest of the cavalry division, Sarah on my back, I thought about what was to come.

I had seen fighting before. But I had never truly been in a real battle. I was excited and scared at the same time. Butterflies flew around my stomach and it took all that I had to stay steady under Sarah's hand.

Most of the men here had never seen a battle. And as I had learned, that was what would make this battle truly exceptional. There were to be more green troops in this battle than there were in almost any other battle. And it would be a scaring experience for most.

There were more men here than I had ever seen before. This was going to be an intense battle, one that would be remembered for years to come.

The land was covered in a purplish-glow from the sun that was beginning to make its way over the horizon. There seemed to be a general hush over the land, even though there were noises everywhere from the men getting ready for battle; bits and spurs clanking, the nervous shuffle of men's feet and the clicking sound of the soldiers checking to make sure that there were bullets in the chambers of their muskets. Our colors flapped in the gentle Tennessee wind, and whisperings traveled from one gray-coated man to the other and through the ranks faster than a message on the telegraph line.

Finally Hardee's portion of the brigade was in order, and it was time to head out. Not a moment too soon either. Johnston had hoped that his battle line would meet the Union soldiers somewhere near six am, but here it was nearly seven o'clock and we hadn't even reached Peabody's camps that were on the outskirts of the large Union encampment.

We marched forward. When the men moved together it seemed as if we were nothing but a sea of butternut gray uniforms. Most of the men were excited to actually see something of a battle, but there were a few that had that sense of foreboding over them like a heavy blanket.

We marched through the hills of the peaceful Tennessee land and toward the place where Peabody's men were camped.

Johnston had wanted his men to be able to surprise the Union soldiers, but by the time we made it to their encampment it was nearly seven-thirty, and the Union soldiers stood at parade-rest in front of their camp.

What a sight we must have been! Thousands of gray-coated soldiers marching slowly, steadily, right toward them, guns and foot-and-a-half bayonets glistening at their sides. It actually excited me a little bit, even though my stomach churned with nervousness. I could feel the expectancy in Sarah as well; her hands shook the slightest bit on the reins and I could tell that she didn't think she was ready for our first real battle.

I started thinking about it. Wait a minute…we could die out here! We had seen and heard of some of the casualties, and we hadn't even been in a "real" battle yet. I shook my head nervously. What *would* happen if Sarah or I were hit by a Federal bullet? How would her family know what happened to her? How would my family know what happened to me?

I put my head down between my knees and shook my head, letting Sarah know how anxious I was. She knew I was scared, but she also knew that fighting for her country was something that she wanted to do, and if she felt that way, I was sure that I would help her accomplish whatever she wanted to do. I would follow her wherever she wanted to go, even if that was straight into the jaws of the thousands of Union soldiers that stood in front of us.

At first, the Union soldiers just kind of stood there and gawked at us. I am sure that they doubted that there was even any Confederate soldiers in the wilderness surrounding their camps, and if there was, there probably was only a few.

They simply weren't able to hold in their surprise.

When we came within range of them, Colonel Shaver called out the command.

"FIRE!"

I heard a sharp bang, too close to my ear as Sarah fired out her first shot, in sync with multiple other shots from the foot soldiers and other members of the cavalry. I jumped for a minute, frightened by the noise, and Sarah steadied me. My eyes began to water from all the smoke; it was so thick that I doubt I was the only one who had any trouble seeing through it. After that, the Confederates let out a Rebel yell that was sure to chill any Yank to the bones, and began to charge forward.

Some of the Federal soldiers shot back, but many fled, scared perhaps by the sheer number of our force, true to their stereotypical yellerbelly nature. The sight of running Bluecoats invigorated the Confederates, and they immediately gave chase, but their encampment had a disorganizing effect on both sides of the battle.

The large Sibley tents scattered the Union soldiers, and the famished Confederates stopped to pillage and raid the tents. It had been, after all, days since many of them had eaten.

At first, Sarah could hardly believe her eyes. She tried to convince some of the other men to keep up their chase. But nothing could stop the mass looting of the Union soldiers' food supply. She soon gave up and dismounted, trying to see if she would be able to get anything in all of the mass confusion going on around her.

The Confederate generals and officers did their best to reorganize their line, but even so, it still took them awhile before the soldiers were in proper order again.

We would be able to wreck this brigade without even putting up too much of a fight. Even though we were dangerously behind schedule, the Yanks still were not prepared for our line to smash into the outskirts of their camp this morning.

When we were reorganized, we continued pushing the Yanks back towards Pittsburg Landing. Shots rang out around us, but the immediate victory gave us courage and we marched forward into the battle.

The cavalry was ordered to the back; since generally cavalry didn't travel with the battle lines itself but rather did little chores like scouting and helping to determine where the lines of infantry and artillery should attack.

We heard the orders from one of the generals—"Back! To the back of the line! Let the infantry and artillery take the front!"

I wondered why we were sent to the back, and if Sarah did as well she didn't say anything about it but turned my nose west and kicked me into a canter with the rest of the little cavalry force.

It was a scene of confusion that was only bound to get a thousand times worse. As I cantered up the hill with Sarah on my back, I tried my best not to trip over any men, guns, or other debris that got in my way, and tried to avoid any low-hanging branches as well.

As we passed the artillery I tried not to look at the nervous horses and mules hauling the heavy cannons. Some of them were already losing their demeanor, rearing and neighing frantically. I shook my head. They weren't even at the battle line yet.

For how well the day had started, one would think that perhaps we would be able to take the Union soldiers easily; that perhaps not so many men would have to die in this battle.

We wouldn't be prepared to see more casualties in this battle than anyone had seen before.

Tucker

After we got over the initial shock of being attacked by thousands of Confederate soldiers and reorganized our lines, the battle really began.

We had been surprised. Somewhat. I am sure that the Confederates had planned a surprise attack, but even so, how could you surprise a Union force of thousands of men, preparing for an attack anyway?

I had seen fights before—shoot, I was in the battle of Pea Ridge already. But I don't think any battle could have prepared me for what I saw at Pittsburg Landing, which would come to be known as the Battle of Shiloh.

The Union soldiers gathered and lined up for a better counter-attack against the Rebs. Once we were near Pittsburg Landing, it was a little easier to maneuver the huge forces against them.

"To the right!"

"Hold your fire!"

"Shoot, shoot!"

The officers yelled commands at their soldiers and the infantry and cavalry did their best to follow them, though it got harder as the battle raged on.

Smoke filled the air; shots rang out constantly. As soon as the artillery got to where they needed to be, the sound of cannons rang out in the already-confusing battlefield.

Later in the day, our soldiers were lined up along a place that would come to be called the "Sunken Road." This road wasn't actually sunken, but it made a good place to form a battle line.

As the day wore on and the sun began to rise higher in the sky, the heat and noise became more and more unbearable. I could hardly keep myself steady as my head spun with all of the noise, and sweat dripped down my ears and into my face as my rider and I continued to dodge bullets. My mouth was dry and tingly; I hadn't had anything to drink since the early morning hours.

It only got worse later in the day. The air was filled with blue smoke from the cannons and gunpowder; so much that it seemed like there was a thick fog over the land, only a much smellier kind of fog. Rebel yells, screeches, and pitiful wails from the wounded wafted around through the smoke, though it was hard to pinpoint exactly where from. Branches whipped my ears and my legs, bullets whizzed around, and the sound of cracking tree limbs could be heard as well.

All I wanted to do was give up. To run away. I didn't care what I had to do; I just wanted to be away from here. But still I fought on. My mother had raised me to be a strong horse. But I didn't think that she could have known just how strong I would have to be.

During a brief lull, I let my mind wander a little. Was this all that I was supposed to be here for? To carry a lieutenant into a man's battle, where all they did was shoot other men, over some petty concern? But it wasn't a petty human concern, I suppose. It was about freedom.

I switched my thoughts over from the battlefield when I could and thought about when we were younger, when Shiloh and I used to fight, mainly, but sometimes we used to be more thoughtful, talking to each other and pondering about the future.

I think we did end up talking about what it would be like to be war-horses. One of our ancestors, after all, was a mount in the Battle of Lexington. If my ancestor could do it, I could do it. I wouldn't want to shame any of my family. I remember telling Shiloh that too. I would never chicken out of a battle, no matter how bad it was, no matter how wounded I was, I would never leave my master.

I couldn't make myself a liar now.

I think that we ended up fighting about who would be the best horse in a battle after that, but it didn't matter now. As much as we fought when we were younger, we still loved each other and hoped that we would stay together for the rest of our days, though that was a bit much to ask for two young Morgan horses who didn't understand a lot about how the human world worked.

I think I had learned a lot in the few short months since I had left Casey's farm.

My thoughts were broken suddenly.

Through the smoke, not even a hundred feet away, a young boy galloped crazily through the mess toward the sunken road line, shooting frantically at anything that was blue-coated and moving.

The horse underneath him was a striking resemblance to my younger brother. Shiloh.

Shiloh

Oh, boy.

When I saw the tall shimmery bay horse held steady under a one-armed general's hand, I thought for sure that it was Tucker. It looked just like him. I shook my head, though, and looked twice when I saw him. There were many bay horses in this war. Hundreds. Maybe even thousands. But not many that were as tall and as well put-together as my brother.

For a minute, I seemed to forget that Sarah was on my back. I turned my body and began to gallop toward the horse. I wanted to talk to him. To hear his voice. If I could do that, I would be able to tell for sure if it was him.

It could have been just the heat getting to me; making me delirious. It was possible.

Men's faces were doused with sweat before they turned black as the thick gunpowder stuck to their faces and turned them dirtier than I think I had ever seen them before. My body was covered in a thick lather of sweat, and I was getting more and more exhausted as I galloped, dodging every bullet that came my way.

But I knew that I had to at least try to get near him, to see if maybe he was my brother. What would happen after that, I wasn't sure.

I whirled, and galloped through the dense tangle of forest and straight toward the Federal battle line on the sunken road. The air was thick with what sounded like buzzing bees, or angry hornets.

But they turned out to be only more bullets, flying in every direction and toward us. Indeed, the area in which we were in would come to be known as the "Hornet's Nest" because of all the whizzing bullets.

Men were falling like leaves all around us, but almost as fast as they fell, more regiments came in to fill their spots.

Sarah screamed—I knew it was she; not only because it was above and directly behind my ears, but because it was a more feminine scream. Not her more practiced Rebel yell or even her "try-to-sound-like-a-boy" yell. This was her sixteen year-old self scream, as her horse that seemed, usually, to be trustworthy balked and then bolted away with her.

She nearly dropped her pistol and yanked on the reins with both hands, harder than I had ever felt her pull before—yank, yank, yank! As far as she was concerned, I was leading her directly to certain death. Fast.

But her needs were put in the back of my mind as I crashed through the forest while still trying to dodge the massive amount of bullets and tree splinters that exploded all around me with each *boom* of the cannon. I needed to get over there.

Clods of dirt flew up under my hooves as I ran, bullets continued to whizz above my ears. Men, horses, and artillery all seemed to work together to get in my way. It seemed to be getting hotter and hotter, I guessed it was because of the fact that I was running with all I was worth. But that wasn't the only reason.

Or really the reason at all. It seemed like some kind of hellfire now.

Finally Sarah regained control, before I was able to get over to the horse that looked like Tucker. I seemed to have his attention though now, as he was looking over in our direction curiously. I let out a thunderous *neigh!* and he neighed back. It sounded a lot like Tucker, and so I really wanted to get over there now.

But there was no way Sarah was letting me get any closer to that line of Yankee soldiers. She pulled one rein to her hip with a uncharacteristic iron-like grip, stopping me in my tracks.

"SHILOH!" she yelled furiously, "Stop!! There's fire!"

I pondered her words for only a second until I looked in the direction where the heat was coming from the strongest.

Sure enough, the parts of the forest that weren't already eaten up by bullets were being licked away by flames, crackling and bursting through the trees and making their way straight toward us.

Tucker

We were losing. The United States of America was losing against a force that we thought was nothing but a few rebels.

The Union forces had realigned near the sunken road, only trying to hold their position as the Confederates sent wave after wave of offence.

I didn't know if the horse I had seen was my brother or not. He had looked just like him, and even came running towards me after I neighed out a greeting. But something had distracted him, and the horse and rider ran away from us. I tried to shake the thought out of my mind that it *was* Shiloh, but no matter how hard I tried, the image of the small gray horse infiltrated my thoughts.

The lieutenant fought on bravely and worked to convince the other soldiers to do the same. But they had the same thoughts that I did. We were losing. Even thought we fought back each time the Confederate soldiers attacked, some of the regiments were already retreating toward the landing. Our position against the sunken road was collapsing as the sun sank lower into the western half of the horizon. General Wallace decided to command the retreat, and after he had done so our force began to shrink, falling back while still attempting to barely fight off the Rebels. Confederates flooded in around us.

Men and horses fled back towards the landing, but we wouldn't be able to find much security there, either. The lieutenant yelled commands at the fleeing men as he tried to make the retreat as dignified as possible. I tried my best to hold steady under the lieutenant's hand and anticipate where he would want me to go, in order to perhaps make his job a little easier.

But it was to no avail. We had almost made it back to the landing when a shot rang out and hit the lieutenant square on. He convulsed and fell from the saddle, landing on the ground in a heap. I stopped and whirled around, even though it took all of my resolve to do so. I couldn't just leave him there.

But I knew he was already gone. And before I could even get to him, a man's hand reached out for my bridle and then leaped on my back, digging spurs into my sides.

It was Ben.

He urged me faster, and on we raced, pushing our way through blue-coated men and horses to get closer to the front of the retreat. When we got closer, we saw an even more disastrous scene before us.

It was complete chaos. Through the thunderous sound of the rushing Tennessee River, wounded men were being loaded onto boats to be ferried to the other side of the huge river for treatment, but the riverbanks were flooded with cowardly soldiers who were attempting to flee across the river as well. The generals were yelling hoarsely at the men, attempting to get them to reorganize. But most of the Union soldiers refused to do so, still attempting to save their own skins. The boats finally dropped their anchors mid-river in order to avoid being swamped by the retreating men.

Grant needed to reorganize for one last stand against the Confederates. If only he could hold out until nightfall. The next day would bring enough reinforcements to win this battle, but only if Grant could keep his army from complete loss.

Finally, Grant was able to organize a line strong enough to hold against an attack from Dill Creek, where most of the

Confederates would be coming from. As it would turn out, there was only one more attack that we would have to stand against.

The Confederates prepared to assault our line one more time. They reorganized and attacked us at our position near the landing as the sun was setting. But it would turn out to be more than they could handle. The exhausted Rebels could hardly hold against us, much less break through our line.

The Confederate leaders ordered their troops to withdraw just before darkness began to settle on the land. Both sides were exhausted to the core and probably wouldn't have been able to fight any more even if they had wanted to.

For me it brought great relief, just as it must have to the men in our ranks. Still, the horror of the battle surrounded us. "Stragglers," as they were called, milled about, still seeking a way to get out of the inevitable battle that would continue tomorrow. The wailing of the wounded and dying could be heard all around us, and the smell of blood and lingering explosives filled my nostrils.

All I wanted to do was rest, but the place was so crowded that men could hardly find a peaceful place to sleep, let alone the horses. And even more men would be arriving throughout the night. Ben looked around at the odd places were horses were tethered, and decided to find me a place to rest farther out from the madness that surrounded us.

He waited for awhile before taking me out, making time to remove the heavy saddle and my bridle, and then brush out my sweat-matted fur, his eyes downcast the entire time.

"I'm sorry, boy," he said while he brushed me. "This ain't right. For horses or for men. Hopefully it'll be all over soon, and before you or I get sent to our Maker."

My legs burned with exhaustion and my entire body was sore from near-hits, tree limbs and branches, and from running into other things on the chaotic battlefield, but I tried to listen to him as he talked.

When he was finally done, he took hold of the rope and led me through the camp, around men and horses and artillery and toward the south side of the camp. “Looks like it’s ‘bout to rain,” he said quietly to me, and I looked up at the sky. Indeed, clouds were beginning to gather and the wind was picking up.

“We really won’t be able to use any of it. It rains so much in this darn country, I can hardly stand it. Not another day of it. But if it’s goin’ to rain, it’s goin’ to rain. And so I have only one other chore to do before it comes.”

I didn’t want to do any more chores, but it really couldn’t be helped. I sighed and followed him, one ear twisted into the conversation as he talked.

“I want to put you near some other horses. In case it does rain, it’ll help reassure you, fellow, if even just a little bit.”

He jumped on my bare back and we went farther into the trees and came to a secluded place maybe a quarter mile from the river, straying far from any regiments that happened to be camped out farther away from the landing.

“Some of the men might think I’m a traitor,” he was saying now, “but I doubt they’ll hold it against me when the find out what I’ve got for it.”

I just wanted to sleep. My head buzzed from the harsh day, and I could have swore that I still heard the cannons firing somewhere in the distance.

But I suddenly became alert when I saw a shadow in the distance. It was a horse and a rider. I became stiff, and raised my head, ready to run if I had to. But Ben was ahead of me. He jumped from my back and covered my nose and mouth with a hand, insisting that I be quiet.

It was hard to do, though, when I saw who it was that he had decided to meet.

It was the short gray horse and the boy I had seen earlier. The boy was short, his white-blonde hair pasted to his head by the sweat and dirt of the day, his clothes dirty beyond recognition. But his pale blue eyes glimmered in the darkness. The short gray horse looked exhausted as well, his coat dirty with brown flecks of mud. I held back a whinny and instead patiently waited until we got close enough to tell in the thick blackness of the night in the forest. The other horse, though, could hardly contain his excitement and pulled away from the boy, trotting toward me.

We touched noses for a second, and I knew it was him. The men watched us quietly for a moment and we were able to talk.

"Shiloh?" I asked tentatively, and he nodded.

"Where have you been, brother? And why are you fighting for the wrong side of this war?" His voice cracked as he asked me, but still, it sounded like relief to my ears. It felt so good to finally hear a familiar voice; one that you had grown up with, and I didn't want to leave.

"Have you got what I asked for?" Ben was asking the younger boy, who came up behind Shiloh.

"Yes—" the boy answered in a rather high-pitched voice, then cleared his throat and started again. "Yep, I got it. Ya got what I wanted in return, Yank?"

"Sure do," he said, and pulled out a small pouch of coffee beans.

The two exchanged their little packages, and thanked each other. Ben looked intently on the boy, but the boy couldn't seem to hold his gaze, and kept looking away from him. It was almost as if Ben wanted to ask the boy a question, maybe a million questions, but something held him back.

Before he could speak, though, the skies opened up and rain began to pour from cloud-laden skies. The short boy turned and grabbed Shiloh's reins, hopping on his short back with ease and galloping away.

Shiloh

When we noticed the fire on the battlefield, we had to turn and run away from the horse that I thought looked like Tucker. I had never seen so much death and destruction around us, and I was hardly able to keep my head straight anymore and succumbed to numbly being directed by Sarah's hands. She lead us back towards a pond a short distance away, one that would later come to be called "Bloody Pond" as wounded soldiers fell into the water to drink and often never came back out of it. At the sight of the pond, Sarah cringed and turned me away. But we couldn't truly run away from any of the scene before us.

We attacked the Union soldiers several more times that day, but we were only able to push them as far back as the landing before night fell upon us.

That night was miserable. Rain kept on pouring. Rain, rain, rain! I hated rain at this point. Would it ever stop?

Our men had it a little better than they had it before at least, feeding on dry rations and staying in the captured Union tents, safe and dry, even if they did complain that the tents leaked a little because of all the bullet holes.

I couldn't believe that I had seen Tucker. My big brother. We had even talked. Ever since seeing him the other day I had a faint glimmer of hope that maybe we would be able to be together again, as he was the only tangible relative I had left. The only living link of life before the war. But I knew now that it was a false hope.

I felt fairly miserable, even though the rest of the troops and horses were in a good mood. Surely we would beat the Yankees tomorrow. Oh, if only we knew what the next day would hold.

I must have gotten an hour's sleep at most when I heard rough men's voices through the rain, not too far from where I was tethered. "Sam!" I heard one of them call out, "hurry up and git yer horse! Colonel Forrest is ordering a scouting trip, not a sleepwalking one."

I started when I saw Sarah at my side. She was no longer in her tattered butternut gray uniform. No way. Now she wore a dirty navy blue Yankee uniform with brass buttons that looked a little big on her; the sleeves rolled up and the bottoms of the pants dragging in the mud. I shuddered when I thought too long about where they got the blue uniforms.

I think for the first time, I began to feel sorry for her. Her face looked so tired that I could even see the dark circles under her eyes through the rain that fell down on us in thick patches. Her feet dragged and she wiped her nose and face much too often. I couldn't stand the thought of her getting sick. I suppose if I was a human, I would probably look about as bad as she did, but there was nothing I could do for her.

I shook subconsciously, spattering water in all directions before Sarah could get the saddle on my back, when I suddenly realized something. I cared for Sarah now. I wanted her to be safe. Though just that simple request seemed to get harder with each passing day as her "adventures" got more dangerous and the battles got more serious. I didn't know what I would do without her, and the thought kind of scared me. But I didn't have time to think on it now.

A small group of men were saddling their horses and preparing to go scouting, directly into the union encampment on the landing to see if they were reinforcing, and how many men were coming into their camp.

What?

That sounded like pure suicide to me. But I had no choice in the matter, and so I let Sarah climb aboard again and we galloped into the rain and straight towards the Union camp.

The tension was so thick in the group of men that one could slice it like a thick chunk of Union cheese. Nobody said anything on the entire trip through the dark, hazy rain. The land was still in the process of cooling down again from the warm spring-like weather, and so a mist-like fog pushed its way up from the ground as we trotted into the darkness.

Nobody joked about the weather, or made comments about the mud, or ridiculed the Yanks in their blue uniforms. We just moved forward as silently as a group of men on horseback was able to.

It was strange to see my men in blue instead of the usual gray, but it only unsettled me a little bit. We were on a mission, and just like all of the other missions we had gone through together, Sarah and I would make it out of there in one piece.

The leader of the group trotted his horse silently across a muddy field, then through the muddy, moccasin-infested Dill Ravine Swamp, through thickly wooded forest and to the top of a bluff. What we saw when we got up there was more frightening then we could have imagined.

There were boats making their way toward the landing where the Union encampment was. One of the boats was already unloading its precious cargo onto the riverbanks.

It was more ranks of blue-coated soldiers. Hundreds and hundreds of Yankees making their way down the gangplank, preparing to whup us tomorrow.

Tucker

The reinforcements came in right on time. Well, still too late for General Grant's liking, but nevertheless they came in time to save us from the destruction that would surely come the next day had we not received them. Rows and rows of men were unloaded from the boats and onto the landing. We would be ready for the battle to continue at dawn the next morning.

But my stomach churned nervously. Not only because of the fear I had for myself, but also now the fear I held for others. Catori. Ben. Shiloh.

Shiloh. I couldn't believe that I had seen him only the day before. I had even talked to him. Even in those few brief minutes, I was able to tell that he missed me. That he wanted to know that I was alright as much as I had wanted to know that he was. But I could also tell that he considered me a traitor. In the few months that we had been separated, he already knew more about the man's war than I did. The disappointment in his face was evident. But what did he have to be disappointed in me for? Why? This wasn't our war, it was like every other human's war. It was one where the horses did as they were told, no matter what the consequences.

When I pictured him, I tried not to think of the horses that lay in the woods or fields, shot down, only waiting for death to relieve them. As I attempted to sleep in the chilly darkness, I tried hard to keep the two pictures apart.

I must have gotten some sleep that night, but it wasn't enough. Before I knew it, Ben was walking through the horses that were tethered in the forest near the camp, currying their soft fur and saddling some of them.

He saddled me, looking even more depressed than he usually did. I knew he didn't want to go back out there. Not back through the dark forest where we would have to maneuver around bodies of men and horses strewn about and among the trees that were eaten up by bullet holes.

Shiloh

Defeat looked certain. Shoot, if I was a darn general or leader or whatever in this battle, I would have turned around right there and made it out of that stupid valley and back to Corinth before the sheer number of Union soldiers swallowed us up.

But Forrest went nuts. He thought that the best way to defeat the Yanks was to attack them before daylight broke, before they had a chance to organize. But the Colonel would have a hard time convincing the leaders of that.

With the surrender of hundreds of blue-coated soldiers the day before, everyone had been quite joyous that night, ignoring the death toll of the day and enjoying what seemed to be the impending defeat of the Federals and the spoils of the day's fighting.

And so there was no night attack. In fact, the Union soldiers nearly surprised *us* on the second day of that battle. There was fighting, fighting, and more fighting. I want to spare the details, partially because I get tired of telling them and partially because it seemed like that was all we did in the few battles that I had taken a part of. *Fight. Shoot. Kill. Repeat.*

I was sick of it. Just waiting for my turn to be shot down. The Yankees attacked our soldiers in waves. Retreat seemed inevitable.

Sarah had managed to stay in the saddle and was furiously shooting at anything that was blue-coated and moved. Rebel yells, screams of the wounded men and grunts of wounded horses, gunshots, cannon shots; everything seemed to pollute the air all at once.

Suddenly I felt Sarah jolt from the saddle. I skidded to a stop and turned toward her.

It was early afternoon. It seemed that we should keep fighting, at least for another four or five hours. But the Confederates were clearly being overwhelmed. They fought like determined dogs though, barely losing each inch of ground in a battle to the death.

"Retreat!"

Finally the call for what seemed to be inevitable.

At first, the men rushed away, but slowly they became more organized.

The Feds realized what the Confederate army was doing, and they chose not to pursue them any further, only whooped and hollered victoriously.

I made my way back to Sarah, dodging bullets the entire time. Well, as skillfully as a horse could, I suppose. What good would I be able to do her if I got shot? But the bullets seemed to be flying less and less, and that made it easier for me to get over to her.

She lay curled on the ground, tears running down the side of her dark face noiselessly. Worry filled my entire body and held me down like a lead weight. Sarah was holding the top of her shoulder, black-red blood leaking through her fingers.

Tucker

Finally! We were victorious! Another battle was won in the west; another Union Victory. But at what cost?

The war generals and leaders of the country would soon find out that more Americans (from the North and South) had died in this single battle than in any other battle that Americans had fought before. The field had been taken easily that day, all of the Confederates had already retreated by the early evening. And it was finally quiet.

I say quiet, but in reality, the absence of gunshots didn't necessarily equal quiet. Any building that was in the area was torn into by bullet holes and used as a camp hospital, including the once-peaceful Shiloh Church building. All day long we could hear the pitiful wailing of those who were wounded. It made for a depressing day.

Ben had suffered minor wounds in the battle, but nothing a good cleaning and a bandage couldn't take care of. He didn't need to see any doctors. The surgeons and nurses were working around the clock to take care of the more seriously wounded soldiers, Confederate captives as well as the Union soldiers.

The land was in despair.

What was once simply a peaceful valley filled with patches of woods and fields became one of the most war-torn areas anyone had ever seen. Bodies were everywhere, along with broken artillery, wagons, and other objects. Somebody would have to clean this mess up, and it was mostly left to the soldiers who were unwounded and able to complete the job. Ben was one of them.

He saddled me up again, early on the morning of the eighth of April. It was a beautiful day, despite all the turmoil that had occurred only hours earlier. Birds were chirping above our heads and the land blossomed with spring. The calming sound of water churning in the creek could be heard now that the blasts had disappeared. It seemed as if the simple beauty of spring was only here to mock us.

A few other soldiers had begun the work of burying the bodies and cleaning up the aftermath of the battle, but Ben wanted to get a better look at the battlefield as a whole and see if there were any wounded horses out there that he would be able to take care of.

"Not many pay attention to the horses," he was telling me as he brushed my fur before throwing the saddle up on my back. "It's generally quite depressing. They're in this war as much as we are, even if they are here against their will. I'm no surgeon. But I can patch up a broken horse and that's what I intend to do."

After he had finished saddling and bridling me, he climbed aboard and kicked me into a trot, which soon turned back into a walk as we had to focus on maneuvering around the piles of bodies and other objects. He looked around, taking in every angle as we walked through what had been a hornet's nest of bullets only the day before.

Most of the horses were dead, many more of them too wounded to be able to recover. It made me sick, and made me want to run away, just to escape what I saw all around me. But if Ben was able to do it, I should be too. Besides, as much as I didn't want to look at the horses that were around, I still wanted to see if Shiloh or Catori might be among those who didn't make it. I shuddered.

We found a limping horse in the depths of the forest, still standing beside his master who had died the night before, hand on his revolver. Ben climbed down and checked if the horse would be able to recover. After testing the leg that the horse was limping on and checking the rest of him, Ben decided that he would be able to fix it back at camp, and so he grabbed the horse's reins and ponied him behind me.

What I saw next surprised me beyond belief. I saw a gray horse ahead in the distance. Immediately I knew it was Shiloh. He was standing next to the river, his head hanging down, reins dragging in the muddy banks of the creek. Mud was smeared on his back legs and his hindquarters, more noticeable because he was such a light-colored horse. His rider lay on the ground, motionless, but breathing.

I yanked the reins in his direction, and Ben turned to look, then he saw it too. He rushed over there, barely stopping me before he jumped off my back.

He crouched down by Shiloh's rider, the young blond boy that I had remembered seeing only a couple nights before when the two had made their surreptitious trade.

He picked the boy up into his lap.

It seemed to be a strange scene. Something rather unexpected in all of the tragedy of war. The tall blue-coated Irish soldier holding the gray-coated boy. The boy seemed to be young, maybe not more than fourteen or fifteen years old, more suited to be a drummer boy than a cavalryman. It saddened me to see someone that young in this war.

It was quiet for a moment; we were far enough away from the hospital area that we no longer heard the noises of the wounded. The only noise seemed to be Shiloh's bridle jangling a little as he put his nose to Ben's head, seemingly asking if his rider was all right.

Ben tore away the gray coat from his shoulder and started at the boy's undershirt. But not before he started to stir. When he looked up and saw Ben, his curly mop of hair and blue uniform, he jumped, removing Ben's hand and trying to scoot away as quickly as possible.

"Hold on there, Johnny Reb," he said as the boy started to squirm. "I'm not going to hurt you. Not now."

The boy continued to squirm a little, before he finally pointed to Ben's canteen and attempted to speak. It came out as a harsh whisper, but Ben could understand. "Water."

Ben raised it up to his lips. "Looks like you've lost a lot of blood, but your wound isn't bad. The doc can have you stitched up in minutes."

The boy shook his head violently. "No!" he nearly shouted. Then, more quietly, "No…you can't do that."

"Why not?" Ben asked, slightly irritated. "You'll be fine. And we don't treat Rebs as bad as we should in the prison camps. And with you being a boy as small as you are, they might just let you go home."

"I can't," he said quietly.

"Why not?" Ben repeated.

"Because," she said, "…I'm a girl."

Shiloh

Believe me, the last person I expected to see come to our rescue was Tucker and that Northern soldier that I had seen only a couple nights before.

It was so strange to see the four of us convene again. We were supposed to be fighting against each other, after all. Sarah's wound wasn't serious, so I knew that she would be alright, as long as somebody would be able to find her. I was unscathed but there was no way that I would leave her now.

I couldn't believe that she had told Ben that she was a girl. She had gone this far in the fight without telling anyone, keeping the secret so well that only her little gray horse would know. But why would she tell now? Was she afraid that a doctor would have been able to find out anyway and sent her home without her horse? Or maybe it was because she seemed to trust Ben way more than she should. Or maybe, it was just because she was tired of fighting. She didn't want to be in this war anymore when she didn't have to be.

But in any event, her secret was spilled. Ben's jaw dropped a little bit, but not as much as you would expect. Perhaps he already sort of knew.

"What do you want me to do then?" he asked her, "you'll lose too much blood if I don't take you to a doctor."

She started to sit up, trying to lean on a tree nearby. "I'm stronger than I look," she said.

"Well that's obvious."

"But I ain't havin' no Yank doctor stitch me up. They'll put me in the prison camp, or send me home, and they'll take my horse."

Ben couldn't really argue with that. "It's just a horse."

"You don't understand. This is my horse. I stole 'im and trained 'im myself. He's my only friend in this blasted war-torn country, and the only one I want to have. I ain't going nowhere if they'll take him away from me."

Ben shook his head. He knew what she meant, but he didn't really know what to do about it.

"Take me to someone who isn't a regular. Or leave me here, I don't care."

"I'm not going to leave you out in the woods with a bullet in your shoulder."

"I don't care. I will die out here, go back to Missouri, or die trying. Don't you know anyone who could help me without rattin' me out?"

Ben started to say something, then stopped, seeming to think about whether or not he should say it. He started again, "well, I, um…well, I can dig bullets out and stitch a little. But I've only worked on horses, so I wouldn't consider myself a regular doctor."

She looked at him with huge, innocent-looking watery blue eyes. "Do it, and do it quickly before the Yanks show up here."

He was able to get the bullet out, and stitch it up. We could only hope that it wouldn't get infected, but time would tell in her case. She took it like a champ though, refusing to let the smallest tear fall out of the corner of her eye while he worked.

When he was done, she laid down for awhile and exhaled quietly. "I need to get out of here."

Ben's eyes looked like he wanted to help her, but he didn't really know how. "How are you going to get out of your service term?"

"It don't bother me one bit. I'm a volunteer, so there's nothing they can do to stop me. I just want to go back home to my family. I'm done with this man's war."

Ben stood up, and paced. He ran his hand along my withers and down my back as he went one way, then the other, thinking. He scratched at his curly mop of hair and sat back down beside her.

"Look," he said, "I'm eighteen years old and I've got two years left of my term. Legally, I can't leave 'til my time is up, regardless of whether or not our men are deserting left and right. I could get in huge trouble for desertion. But I've heard most of your story, and I think that after all you've been through, I can't leave you to go all the way back to Missouri by yourself, not with all the violence that's been going on. Everywhere. I'll take you back."

He stopped suddenly when he heard crashing in the woods a short distance away. More soldiers were coming through, and undoubtedly they were Northern ones. He had to make up his mind.

He quickly pulled Shiloh around and tied his reins to my saddle in order to pony him. He looked at Sarah for a minute before he grabbed her in his strong arms and put her atop my back, then jumped up behind her. He kicked me into a run, and we took off, loping toward the north and the west.

Shiloh

Ben wasn't sure about leaving his regiment. He wasn't sure about how proper it would be to be traveling alone with a girl who was only a few years younger than he. Ben wasn't sure about a lot of things, but at this point he seemed to be following his heart more than his head. And I was sure glad for it. Sarah and I probably wouldn't have been able to make it very far if it wasn't for him.

We rode for a long while before we were able to find a place where they would let Sarah rest and help her recover that was a good distance away from the battlefield. The family that lived there knew some of Ben's family, and fortunately for us the people were willing to let us stay. The old man who was there tried to convince Ben that it was his duty to return to the battlefield but Ben wouldn't have any of it. He was the one who had found her and brought her to the man's house, and he would see it all the way through until he was able to get Sarah back home. He knew it was risky though, and so we only spent a few days there, until Sarah was at least able to ride without a lot of pain. We set out at sunrise, heading north again over vast expanses of prairie intertwined with thick tangles of forest along the riverbeds.

"Where exactly is it that you call home in Missouri?" Ben asked softly as we trotted along.

"Just a ways out of Nevada City," she explained, "it's close to Fort Scott and only a few miles away from the Kansas Border. My folks' place will be just a couple miles outside of it."

Ben nodded, looking down at the ground beneath Tucker's strong forefeet. The spring was warm and mild, and the quiet breeze blowing across the prairie seemed so very calm compared to the battle that had been raging only a few days before.

Sarah's hair had continued to grow out around her face, the whitish-blond hair falling into her eyes and down the back of her neck. It would only be awhile until she looked fully female again. Every once in awhile I seemed to sense her stealing glances at Ben and saw him look back. I suppose he *was* handsome in a girl's eyes: tall, thin and tough as nails, with a hard-set jaw but gentle brown eyes. They seemed to flirt back and forth but at the same time they seemed to deny it. I think that perhaps they had known each other longer than either Tucker or I could know.

We traveled for miles, for days. It hadn't seemed like such a journey when we went south as we usually only traveled a short distance every day and for the fact that it had seemed more broken out with raids and the other missions that we needed to accomplish along the way.

Day by day we seemed to bond closer though. It seemed odd to me that we were ever apart. That Ben and Sarah were ever apart. And that there was an entire war that kept us separated.

Soon enough though, we could see where Nevada City was up on the horizon. It wouldn't be long before we were there, and not long after that before we would be to Sarah's parents' home. Sarah hesitated for a minute. It didn't look right.

"Giddyup!" Sarah dug her heels into my sides and we loped down along a trail and towards the town.

We didn't even have to get very close before she realized what was going on. There was no more downtown. There was no courthouse. No churches, no houses. There was no more city. Sarah's hometown was burned to the ground.

Tucker

Sarah didn't say anything but slipped to the ground from Shiloh's back. The black charred remains were the only thing that stood up against the early Missouri sky. Everything was gone.

Ben and I loped up behind her. Sarah was still speechless.

Ben didn't know what to say at first.

"Bushwhackers?" he asked softly.

Sarah turned around with a fury in her eyes. "Bushwhackers?" she said, then laughed quietly. "Nevada is the 'Bushwhacker Capital of the World.' They wouldn't destroy it. Not a single person in this entire town even voted for Lincoln.

"This ain't no Bushwhacker's mess. This ain't no Missourian's mess, no Jayhawker mess." She walked up closer to Ben, brave enough to jab a finger into his chest. "This is all the Yanks' fault! Those stupid, blue-coated, yellowbellies! It's gotta be something to do with that General Order 11—" she stopped abruptly when she thought of something. "The order!"

She grabbed Shiloh's reins and jumped on his back, galloping away. Ben quickly did the same and we galloped after her. It didn't take me long to catch up to Shiloh, since I still was faster than he was, but my brother had gotten a lot quicker in the months that we had been separated. I let him gallop ahead still, as I had no clue where we were going.

We finally came to another place out in the country. A little farmstead it appeared to be. Or at least what used to be a little farmstead. What appeared now were the charred remains of a barn. A house. Black burnt stubs that used to be an apple orchard.

Once again Sarah slid off Shiloh's back. Ben stayed behind, holding the reins loosely. For what must have been about five minutes, but seemed like an eternity, the only sounds were that of the gentle Missouri wind and Shiloh quietly chomping his metal bit. Sarah had her back turned to us, still wearing the Confederate garb that she had fought in only a few weeks ago. She pulled off her wide-brimmed rebel hat, then dropped it on the ground. The wind tousled our manes and her hair while Ben sat and watched, unmoving.

She finally turned around, tears brimming at her pale blue eyes. Ben moved me beside Shiloh, then dismounted. Both of us bowed our heads respectfully, one of us wearing the saddle and bridle of the United States army, the other of the Confederate States of America. Ben took off his navy blue cap and wrung it in his hands nervously, then stood beside her. She looked up at him.

"What am I going to do?"

He had no answer, but looked down and gently took her hand in his.

Epilogue

The war was far from over. Little did we know that there would still be three entire years of the bloody battles, in the East as well as the West.

Ben did return to his regiment as soon as he was able to. Though he was nervous; he found out that so many men had deserted in the Battle of Shiloh that there wasn't much punishment dished out to those who came back. He continued on to fight many battles with Tucker at his side.

Sarah was devastated to find her entire hometown burned to the ground as well as her family's farm. Federal soldiers had been ordered to burn the town of Nevada, Missouri because of all the guerilla violence that was perpetuated there. But many other people would have to pay the same price or greater in a nation torn by war, especially in the Border States like Missouri. Sarah's family was spared, but because she didn't know where they were, she agreed to spend a few months with Ben's sister in Minnesota.

I spent some time pulling artillery in the U.S. Army until I was able to join Sarah in Minnesota where we both patiently waited for the war to come to an end, to be able to see Ben and Tucker again.

Luckily, sometime after the Battle of Gettysburg, both returned home safe and sound. Many were not as fortunate, as thousands would have to die before the bloody war would come to an end.

Sarah did not return to the battlefield. Though she was as courageous as any man or boy, she couldn't bring herself to fight again after all the death and destruction she had witnessed in the Battle of Shiloh.

Ben and Sarah were married soon after the war was over and decided to start a new life out west. Sarah was able to find her family before the war ended and kept in constant contact with them, though her two older brothers died fighting for the Confederacy. After Ben and Sarah settled down, Tucker and I spent our days pulling buggies and farm equipment while getting sleek and fat on good grain, like horses should.

Both Tucker and I had learned quite a bit fighting on opposite sides of the war, I think. Take every day as it comes, because you don't really know if it could be your last. Fight for what you believe in. Sometimes war is not as clear-cut as you'd think. Though Tucker and I fought in two different worlds—different people, different values, different *countries*—we were still the same horses. We had changed a lot since we fought as colts in the meadow, but we were still brothers, just as we always were.

Blast from the Past

What do most people think of when they think of the American Civil War? Slavery? Gettysburg? Sumter or Antietam?

Sometimes our eyes glaze over when we hear about the American Civil War. We have heard it all before. Lincoln, slavery, the blue versus the gray.

But there are so many aspects of the Civil War that many people don't know about or know little about.

One such thing is the many battles that went on in the western theater of the Civil War. While many great battles were won and lost in the East, there were many intense battles and violence in the West. Writing a historical novel about the Civil War could be taken many different ways and could explore many different aspects of the lives and events of the war, but I chose to center around the Battle of Shiloh in Southwestern Tennessee.

The Battle of Shiloh was one of the most prominent battles in the West. It took place April 6-7, 1862. One of the most outstanding facts about the battle was the amount of sheer casualties. There were more than 23,000 Union and Confederate casualties in the two-day battle, one of the greatest casualty counts Americans had ever seen at the time. The battle was significant because most people thought at the beginning of the war that it would be over soon with few casualties. Shiloh easily proved otherwise. It was also a decisive battle in the western theater. After the Confederate losses of Fort Donelson and Fort Henry, their loss at Shiloh helped turn the Border States' opinions against the Confederacy.

Another perspective many people don't know much about is the Southerners', especially those in the Border States such as Missouri and Kansas. The soldiers and men of the Confederate South are usually portrayed as cruel, slave-owning brutes.

Though there were many plantations and slave owners in the South, they were vastly outnumbered by those who didn't own slaves. More than *seventy percent* of white males living in the Confederate states did not own any slaves at all, and less than one percent owned more than fifty, the general requirement of a large-scale plantation. Most men who fought for the south honestly thought that it was only over state's rights, some going as far as to say that it was a kind of "second revolution," and that they were protecting the rights that their forefathers fought to obtain. It is this kind of thinking that I tried to capture in Sarah's mind, while at the same time refusing to accept slavery in any way as right. Sarah was like a typical young Southerner at the time, naïve and either unaware of slavery's effects or unnoticing.

I brought Nevada, Missouri into the book as well after I spent a couple years there going to college and became intrigued with the town's history. Nevada was known as the "Bushwhacker Capital of the World" because of all the Bushwhackers and violence in the area. Missouri in general was very violent before and during the war. General Order Eleven was issued by Union General Thomas Ewing, and it demanded all people in a few western counties of Missouri to evacuate, to help dissipate some of the violence. The burning of the town by Union soldiers happened in 1863 but I brought it in the book earlier to help with the time frame.

Many people haven't heard that women fought in Civil War battles as well. Did you know that historians estimate that more than 400 women disguised themselves as men and fought in the Civil War? Though the home was still considered a woman's place during this time period, many women disregarded these stereotypes and worked for the cause, most nursing the sick and wounded, cooking or sewing clothes for the soldiers. But some took it to the next level, disguising themselves and fighting next to their brothers and husbands, or just fighting for a cause that they believed in. It was easier to do in the 1800's than one would expect—all ranks generally wore loose, baggy clothing, the inability to grow facial hair would often be attributed to youthfulness, and soldiers slept clothed and bathed separately. Women fought in nearly every major Civil War battle, including the Battle of Shiloh. So perhaps my fictional story of Tucker, Shiloh, Ben and Sarah might not be so far off after all.

The name "Shiloh" came from the small church that was located near the battlefield. Ironically, "Shiloh" means "Place of Peace" in Hebrew.

Shiloh, the battle and the fictional character, was anything but. Shiloh and Tucker were both Morgan horses, a breed that would have been a good fit for what soldiers were looking for in the Civil War. The Morgan horse was one of the earliest breeds of horse developed in the United States. All Morgan horses generally trace back to a horse owned by a man named Justin Morgan, who received a horse for a payment of a debt and called him Figure. Soon after his horse, as well as the horses descended from his horse, became known as Morgan horses. Morgan horses are known mainly for their versatility, but also for their good looks, athleticism, and temperament, making them an excellent mount for cavalry units in the Civil War.

A typical mount and a Union soldier during the Civil War Period. (Photo courtesy of The Library of Congress)

Just like my other historical fiction books—the historical details of *Day and Night* are not one hundred percent historically accurate and are not intended to be. For example, the timeline of the story is condensed in some parts and lengthened in others in order to better fit the purpose of my novel. Places have been made closer to each other in order for the characters to travel to and from them in a more timely manner. Exact dates have been altered slightly and names have been changed. But the heart of the story is true: the struggle of a nation torn apart by a Civil War.

Bibliography/For Further Reading: Books used in the writing of *Day and Night* as well as the *Blast From the Past* Section

Armistead, Gene C. *Horses and Mules in the Civil War: A Complete History with a Roster of More than 700 War Horses*. Jefferson, NC: McFarland, 2013. Print.

Brophy, Patrick. *Three Hundred Years: Historical Highlights of Nevada and Vernon County, Missouri*. Boulder, CO: D.G. Logan, DGL Info Write, 1993. Print.

Cottrell, Sue. *Hoof Beats North and South: Horses and Horsemen of the Civil War*. Hicksville, NY: Exposition, 1975. Print.

Cunningham, Edward, Gary D. Joiner, and Timothy B. Smith. *Shiloh and the Western Campaign of 1862*. New York: Savas Beatie, 2009. Print.

DiMarco, Louis A. *War Horse: A History of the Military Horse and Rider*. Yardley, PA: Westholme, 2008. Print.

Earle, Jonathan Halperin, and Diane Mutti Burke. *Bleeding Kansas, Bleeding Missouri: The Long Civil War on the Border*. N.p.: n.p., n.d. Print.

Foote, Shelby. *Shiloh: A Novel*. New York: Vintage, 1991. Print.

Frank, Joseph Allan., and George A. Reaves. *"Seeing the Elephant": Raw Recruits at the Battle of Shiloh*. New York: Greenwood, 1989. Print.

Hall, Richard. *Patriots in Disguise: Women Warriors of the Civil War*. New York: Paragon House, 1993. Print.

Hardee, William Joseph. *Hardee's Rifle and Light Infantry Tactics ...* New York: J.O. Kane, 1862. Print.

"History." *City of Nevada*. City of Nevada, 2013. Web. 9 Dec. 2014.

"History of the American Morgan Horse." *American Morgan Horse Association*. American Morgan Horse Association, n.d. Web. 13 Jan. 2015.

Kunkel, Jack. *The Battle of Shiloh: A Step-by-Step Account of One of the Greatest Battles of the Civil War*. N.p.: Pepper, 2012. Print.

Linderman, Gerald F. *Embattled Courage: The Experience of Combat in the American Civil War*. New York: Free, 1987. Print.

McPherson, James M. *Battle Cry of Freedom: The Civil War Era*. New York: Oxford UP, 1988. Print.

Righthand, Jess. "The Women Who Fought in the Civil War." *Smithsonian*. Smithsonian Magazine, 7 Apr. 2011. Web. 14 Oct. 2014.

Smith, Sam. "Female Soldiers in the Civil War." *Council on Foreign Relations*. Council on Foreign Relations, n.d. Web. 24 August. 2014.

About the Author

Mattie Richardson is 21 years old, has hair that's the color of the sunset, and a desire to be anything but ordinary. She wrote her first book, *Appaloosy*, when she was thirteen years old and published it when she was sixteen. Since then, she's published four other books, *Dusty's Trail*, *Golden Sunrise*, *Blackberry Blossom* and *Day and Night.* In December of 2011 she graduated high school early and began her first semester of college in January.

Author Mattie Richardson on a historic adventure

After finishing her first two years of college and earning her associate's degree, she came to a crossroads in her own life and decided to take a break from school. She currently works fulltime at a local business, in-between writing and daydreaming about the day she can become a full-time author and adventurer.

Though she can never find enough time for her writing, she still enjoys writing her historical fiction horse stories and other novels, making history fun for students and adults alike. When she's not working on her studies or writing, she enjoys riding and training horses, playing fiddle, guitar, and drums, speaking to schools and other groups about her books and writing,

as well as typesetting and editing others' books.
No matter how busy Mattie gets, she will always make time for reader comments and questions. Feel free to write to her at the address found on the order form at the end of this book.

Other Books By Mattie Richardson

Appaloosy

Storm is a beautiful brown Appaloosa stallion belonging to the famous Nez Perce Tribe. He hates living the domesticated life and is determined to escape and run free acoss the open west with a wild herd. Instead, he is given to a young brave named White Feather, and surprisingly, the two bond together as everlasting friends. But when war breaks out in the Idaho wilderness, Storm's life is turned upside-down. He is captured and taken to live with white men. After being sold twice and facing many unique challenges, he comes to live with Faith, a young girl living on a small farm with her family. The two soon become inseparable, and Storm was content to live with her for the rest of his days. But when he is stolen by rustlers heading west, once again circumstances have spun his life around.

When he is finally able to free himself, he must decide between returning to Faith….or the chance to be free.

Dusty's Trail

WANTED:

YOUNG, SKINNY WIRY FELLOWS NOT OVER 18. MUST BE EXPERT RIDERS WILLING TO RISK DEATH DAILY. ORPHAN PREFERED. WAGES $25 PER WEEK.

When young Levi Anderson reads this ad in a local newspaper, he can hardly resist the urge to saddle up and head out for a new job.

Trouble is, his horse Dusty doesn't think it's such a good idea.

Dusty enjoys his quiet life working on Levi's small family ranch; taking Levi to town, chasing cows, fixing fence and sometimes even horseracing with the neighbors. He couldn't imagine leaving.
Levi steals away in the middle of the night, taking the reluctant Dusty along with him. Dusty may sometimes rear and buck, gallop and balk, but he tries to be good and really is in with his friend and rider Levi for the long run. And the more they gallop on those wild runs with the "Pony Mail," the closer they bond as friends. But when Indian trouble arises, endangering the Pony Express Stations and even Levi's life, with Dusty prove to be a worthy mount?

Golden Sunrise
Cheyenne is a beautiful golden Palomino mare raised in Northern Texas during the early 1800's.
When her owner, Jared, is convinced to become a volunteer soldier for the emerging Texas fight for independence, she must travel with him along with his friend Rueben in to San Antonio, Texas. Jared has orders to help defend the famous Fort Alamo against Mexican forces, and the more Cheyenne learns about Texas' fight for independence; he more the feisty mare is determined to help Jared fight in any way she can. Along the way the two fight in battles, hide a cannon near the town of Gonzalez, and meet new friends like James Bowie and the famous Davy Crockett.
But the Mexican forces are set on extinguishing the fire of Texan independence in any way they can…will Jared and Cheyenne make it through the war? And will the Texas flag fly for freedom?

Blackberry Blossom

It takes a lot of hard work and dedication to play the fiddle. But at sixteen, Molly is already a master. After running away from home she finds that the best way to survive in America's great depression days is to travel around offering fiddle performances in exchange for money, food, or even just a place to stay. She loves her nomadic lifestyle, with no one to tell her what to do or where to go, and she wouldn't trade the way she lives for anything.

Traveling east from the area known as the "dust bowl," she meets Pepper, a lanky boy about her age who plays guitar and has a great sense of humor. The two agree to be partners and continue to travel east, performing in cafes and theaters as well as "Hoovervilles" and shanty towns.

Their adventures take them all over the country, but as they become more well-known, the more trouble they encounter. Will the two be able to keep playing their instruments, riding the rails, and meeting new people every day, continuing their adventurous lifestyle? Or is there something bigger for them that they never could have imagined?

Coming Soon

The Secret of the Hemlock Forest

Sunshine is just an ordinary girl. Living an ordinary life, going to an ordinary school, facing ordinary obstacles of the ordinary fourteen year-old…like what clothes to wear, how to make friends, or what she should do Saturday night. The only thing that sets her apart from the others is that she often spends time alone in the hemlock forest near her home. People wonder why she spends her time there—there are stories told of people going into the forest and never coming out again, about crazy people and animals that live there, or other strange happenings. There are fables and legends about the creatures that live there.

The forest is rarely visited. By humans, anyway. Maybe there is a real reason why people don't go into the forest. But Sunshine just sits and relaxes within the realms of the dark forest, thinking about the creatures that were said to live there, and contemplating just how ordinary and unsocial she really is.

But when she hears a strange sobbing in the woods one evening she couldn't help but follow the sound. What she stumbles across is something unusual; something that may even teach her a lesson about her own life…something extraordinary.

Crazy 8

Life is hard growing up in a small town. It's even harder if you're grown up in what's known as the crazy family with eight kids!

Okay, maybe not everyone knows us as “crazy,” but having seven siblings is always more fun, because life is never boring. I got used to growing up as the one that always stood out. Between my status as the oldest, my crazy red hair, and my desire to always make the best out of whatever situation I found myself in, I learned to go with whatever hand I was dealt and realize that things won’t always work out the way that you wanted them to.

Being an author is hard too. But having seven siblings almost guarantees that I never will run out of material! Many of the ideas and scenarios that I placed in my five published novels and dozens more unpublished stories started as situations that happened at home—and now I bring some unfiltered, goofy stories from our lives into your hands.

Eight stories come together to make a compilation that may not make me the most popular person in the world with most people (or with my parents!), but hey, what ever did?

ORDER FORM

Use this convenient order form to order more books (signed!) by Mattie Richardson, or order them online at Amazon.com®

PLEASE PRINT:

NAME:___________________________________

ADDRESS:________________________________

CITY:____________________**STATE:**__________

ZIP:_______________

PHONE:_________________________________

_____Copy (ies) of *Appaloosy* @ 7.95 each = $_________

_____ Copy (ies) of *Dusty's Trail* @ 7.95 each= $_________

_____ Copy (ies) of *Golden Sunrise* @ 7.95 each = $_________

_____ Copy(ies) of *Day and Night* @ 7.95 each= $__________

____Copy(ies) of *Blackberry Blossom* @ 9.95 each=$________

Postage: $2.55 for the first book, $1.00 for each additional book:

$________

Total amount enclosed: $_______

Send order form and check or money order payable to Mattie Richardson at:

Mattie Richardson
5749 139th Ave. SE
Sheldon, ND 58068

Thank You!